Cain

José Saramago

Cain

TRANSLATED FROM THE PORTUGUESE
BY MARGARET JULL COSTA

Harvill Secker
LONDON

Published by Harvill Secker 2011

2 4 6 8 10 9 7 5 3 1

© José Saramago & Editorial Caminho, SA, Lisbon 2009
by arrangement with Literarische Agentur Mertin, Inh. Nicole Witt e.K.,
Frankfurt am Main, Germany

English translation copyright © Margaret Jull Costa 2011

First published with the title *Caim* in 2009
by Editorial Caminho, SA, Lisbon

First published in Great Britain in 2011 by
HARVILL SECKER
Random House
20 Vauxhall Bridge Road
London SW1V 2SA

www.randomhouse.co.uk

Addresses for companies within The Random House Group Limited can be found at:
www.randomhouse.co.uk/offices.htm

The Random House Group Limited Reg. No. 954009

A CIP catalogue record for this book is available from the British Library

ISBN 9781846554469 (hardback)
ISBN 9781846555435 (trade paperback)

This publication was assisted by a grant from the Direcção-Geral do Livro
e das Bibliotecas / Portugal

MINISTÉRIO DA CULTURA

DG
LB

DIRECÇÃO-GERAL
DO LIVRO E DAS
BIBLIOTECAS

The Random House Group Limited supports The Forest Stewardship Council (FSC), the
leading international forest certification organisation. All our titles that are printed on Greenpeace
approved FSC certified paper carry the FSC logo. Our paper procurement policy can be found at
www.randomhouse.co.uk/environment

Mixed Sources

Product group from well-managed
forests and other controlled sources

FSC www.fsc.org Cert no. TT-COC-2139
© 1996 Forest Stewardship Council

Typeset by Palimpsest Book Production Limited
Falkirk, Stirlingshire

Printed and bound in Great Britain by
CPI Mackays, Chatham, ME5 8TD

For Pilar, of course

By faith Abel offered unto God a more excellent sacrifice than Cain, by which he obtained witness that he was righteous, God testifying of his gifts: and by it he being dead yet speaketh.

Hebrews 11:4
Book of Nonsense

1

When the lord, also known as god, realised that adam and eve, although perfect in every outward aspect, could not utter a word or make even the most primitive of sounds, he must have felt annoyed with himself, for there was no one else in the garden of eden whom he could blame for this grave oversight, after all, the other animals, who were, like the two humans, the product of his divine command, already had a voice of their own, be it a bellow, a roar, a croak, a chirp, a whistle or a cackle. In an access of rage, surprising in someone who could have solved any problem simply by issuing another quick fiat, he rushed over to adam and eve and unceremoniously, no half-measures, stuck his tongue down the throats of first one and then the other. From the texts which, over the centuries, have provided a somewhat random record of those remote times, be it of events that might, at some future date, be awarded canonical status and others deemed to be the fruit of apocryphal and irredeemably heretical imaginations, it is not at all clear what kind of tongue was being referred to here, whether the moist, flexible muscle that moves around in the buccal cavity and occasionally outside it too, or the gift of speech, also known as language, that the lord had so regrettably forgotten to give them and about which we know nothing, since not a trace of it remains, not even a heart engraved on the bark of a tree, accompanied by some sentimental message, something along the lines of I love eve. It's likely that the lord's violent assault on his offspring's silent tongues had another motive, namely, given that, in principle, you can't have one without the other, that of putting them in contact with the deepest depths of their physical being, the so-called perturbations of the inner self, so that, in future, they could, with some authority, speak of those dark and labyrinthine disquiets out of whose window, the mouth, they were already peering. Well, anything is possible. With the praiseworthy scrupulousness of any skilled craftsman, making up with due humility for his earlier negligence, the lord wanted to make sure that his mistake had been corrected, and so he asked adam, What's your name, and the man replied, I'm adam, your first-born. Then the creator turned to the woman, And what is your name, I'm Eve, the first lady, she replied rather unnecessarily, since there was no other. The lord was satisfied and bade farewell with a fatherly See you later, then, and went about his business. And, for the first time, adam said to eve, Let's go to bed.

Seth, their third child, will only come into the world one hundred and thirty years later, not because his mother's womb required that amount of time to complete the fabrication of a new descendant, but because the gonads of father and mother, the testes and ovaries respectively, had taken more than a century to mature and to develop sufficient generative power. It must be pointed out to our more impatient readers, first, that the fiat was given once and once only, second, that men and women are not sausage machines, and, third, that hormones are very complicated things, they can't just be produced from one day to the next, nor can they be found in pharmacies or supermarkets, you have to let matters take their course. Before seth came into the world, cain had already arrived, followed, shortly afterwards, by abel. By the way, one must not underestimate the intense boredom of all those years spent without neighbours, without distractions, without some small child crawling about between kitchen and living room, with no other visitors but the lord, and even his visits were few and very brief, interspersed by long intervals of absence, ten, fifteen, twenty, fifty years, so we can easily imagine that the sole occupants of that earthly paradise must have felt like poor orphans abandoned in the forest of the universe, not that they would have been able to explain what the words orphan and abandoned meant. It's true that every now and then, although again not with any great frequency, adam would say to eve, Let's go to bed, but their conjugal routine, aggravated, in their case, due to inexperience, by the complete lack of alternative positions to adopt, proved to be as destructive as an invasion of woodworm to a roof beam. You hardly notice anything from the outside, just a little dust here and there falling from tiny holes, but, inside, it's quite a different matter, and the collapse of something that had seemed so sturdy will not be long in coming. In such situations, there are those who say that a child can have an enlivening effect, if

3

not on the libido, which is the work of chemicals far more complex than merely learning how to change a nappy, then at least on feelings, which, you must admit, is no small gain. As for the lord and his sporadic visits, the first was to see if adam and eve had had any problems setting up house, the second to find out what benefits they had gleaned from their experience of country life and the third to warn them that he would not be back for a while, because he had to do the rounds of the other paradises that exist in the heavens. Indeed, he would not appear again until much later, on a date that has not been recorded, in order to expel the unhappy couple from the garden of eden for the heinous crime of having eaten of the fruit of the tree of the knowledge of good and evil. This episode, which gave rise to the first definition of a hitherto unknown concept, original sin, has never been satisfactorily explained. Firstly, even the most rudimentary of intelligences would have no difficulty in grasping that being properly informed about something is always preferable to being ignorant, especially in such delicate matters as good and evil, which could put anyone at risk, quite unwittingly, of being consigned to eternal damnation in a hell that had not yet been invented. Secondly, the lord showed a lamentable lack of foresight, because if he really didn't want them to eat that fruit, it would have been easy enough simply not to have planted the tree or to have put it somewhere else or surrounded it with barbed wire. Thirdly, it wasn't because they had disobeyed god's instructions that adam and eve discovered they were naked. They were already stark naked when they went to bed, and if the lord had never noticed such an evident lack of modesty, the fault must lie with a father's blindness, an apparently incurable infliction that prevents us from seeing that our children are, after all, neither better nor worse than all the others.

A point of order. Before we continue with this instructive and definitive history of cain, undertaken with unprecedented boldness, it might be advisable to introduce some clarity into the chronology of events. So, let us begin by clearing up certain malicious doubts about adam's ability to make a child when he was one hundred and thirty years old. At first sight, if we stick to the fertility indices of modern times, no, he clearly wouldn't, but during the world's infancy, those same one hundred and thirty years would have represented a vigorous adolescence that not even the most precocious of casanovas would have sneered at. It is, moreover, worth remembering that adam lived until he was nine hundred and thirty years old, thus narrowly missing being drowned in the great flood, for he died when lamech was still alive, lamech being the father of noah, the future builder of the ark. He would, therefore, have had the time and leisure to make all the children he did make and many more if he had so wished. As we said earlier, adam's second child, born after cain, was abel, a handsome, fair-haired boy, who, having been the object of the best proofs of the lord's esteem, met a very sticky end indeed. The third child, as we also said, was called seth, but he will not form part of this narrative, which we are writing step by step with all the meticulousness of a historian, and so we'll leave him here, just a name and nothing more. There are those who say that the idea of creating a religion was born in his head, but we have given abundant attention to such ticklish matters in the past, with reprehensible levity, according to some experts, and in terms that will doubtless prove deleterious to us when it comes to the final judgement at which everyone will be condemned, either for doing too much or too little. We are only interested now in the family of which father adam is the head, although he proved to be a very bad head, and we really can't put it any other way, since all it took was for his wife to offer him the forbidden fruit of the knowledge of good and evil and our illogical first patriarch, after a certain amount of persuasion, more for appearance's sake than out of any real conviction, duly choked on it, leaving us men marked for ever by that irritating piece of apple that will neither go up nor down. There are also those who say that the reason adam didn't manage to swallow the whole of that fateful fruit was because the lord suddenly turned up, demanding to know what was going on. Now before we forget about it completely or before our continuation of the story renders the fact redundant because it comes too late, we will tell you about the stealthy, almost clandestine visit the lord made to the garden of eden one hot summer night. As usual, adam and eve were sleeping, naked, beside each other, not touching, a deceptively edifying image of the most perfect innocence. They did not wake up, and the lord did not wake them either. He had gone there with the intention of correcting a slight flaw, which, as he had finally realised, seriously marred his creations, and that flaw, can you believe it, was the lack of a navel. The pale skin of his babies, untouched by the gentle sun of paradise, was too naked, too vulnerable, and in a way obscene, if that word existed then. Quickly, in case they should wake up, god reached out and very lightly pressed adam's belly with the tip of his forefinger, making a rapid circling movement, and there was a navel. The same procedure, carried out on eve, produced similar results, with the one important difference that her navel was much better as regards design, shape and the delicacy of its folds. This was the last time that the lord looked upon his work and saw that it was good.

Fifty years and one day after this fortunate surgical intervention, which gave rise to a new era in the aesthetics of the human body under the consensual motto that everything about it can always be improved, disaster struck. With a crack of thunder, the lord appeared. He was dressed differently from usual, in keeping perhaps with what would become the new imperial fashion in heaven, wearing a triple crown on his head and wielding a sceptre as if it were a cudgel. I am the lord, he cried, I am he. A mortal silence fell over the garden of eden, not a sound, not even the buzz of a wasp, the barking of a dog, the trilling of a bird, or the trumpeting of an elephant. Nothing, only the chattering of a flock of starlings that had congregated in a leafy olive tree, there since the garden was first created, and which suddenly took flight as one, so many, hundreds, if not thousands of them, that they nearly obscured the sky. Who has disobeyed my orders, who has eaten of the fruit of my tree, asked god, fixing adam with a look that can only be described as coruscating, a word which, though highly expressive, has sadly fallen out of use. In desperation, the poor man tried in vain to swallow the tell-tale piece of apple, but his voice refused to come out, neither fore nor aft. Answer, said the angry voice of the lord, who was brandishing his sceptre in a most threatening manner. Plucking up his courage, and conscious of how wrong it was to put the blame on someone else, adam said, The woman you gave to be with me, she gave me the fruit of that tree and I did eat. The lord turned on the woman and asked, What is this that you have done, The serpent beguiled me and I did eat, Liar, deceiver, there are no serpents in paradise, Lord, I did not say that there were serpents in paradise, but I did have a dream in which a serpent appeared to me, saying, So god has forbidden you to eat the fruit of every tree in the garden, and I said no, that wasn't true, that the only tree whose fruit we could not eat was the one that grows in the middle of paradise, for we would die if we touched it, Serpents can't speak, at most they hiss, said the lord, The serpent in my dream spoke, And may one know what else the serpent said, asked the lord, trying to give the words a mocking tone that ill accorded with the celestial dignity of his robes, The serpent said that we wouldn't die, Oh, I see, the lord's irony was becoming more and more marked, it would seem that this serpent thinks he knows more than I do, That is what I dreamed, my lord, that you didn't want us to eat of that fruit because we would open our eyes and know good and evil just as you know them, lord, And what did you do, you fallen, frivolous woman, when you woke from this delightful dream, I went straight to the tree, ate the fruit and brought some back for adam, who also ate, It got stuck just here, said, adam, touching his throat, Right, said the lord, if that's the way you want it, that's the way it shall be, from now on you can bid farewell to the good life, you, eve, will not only suffer all the discomforts of pregnancy, morning sickness included, you will give birth in pain, and yet you will still feel desire for your husband, and he shall rule over you, Poor me, said eve, what a bad beginning, and what a sad fate will be mine, You should have thought of that before, and as for you, adam, the ground is cursed because of you, and in sorrow will you eat of it all of your days, it will bring forth only thorns and thistles, and you will have to eat the herbs of the fields, only by the sweat of your brow will you manage to grow enough to eat, until you return to the ground out of which you came, wretched adam, for dust you are and to dust you will return. That said, the lord plucked out of the air a couple of animal skins to cover the nakedness of adam and eve, who exchanged knowing winks, for they had known they were naked from the very first day and had made the most of it too. Then the lord said, In knowing good and evil, man has become like a god, and if you were to eat of the fruit of the tree of life you would gain eternal life, whatever next, two gods in one universe, that is why I am expelling you and your wife from the garden of eden, at whose gate I will place an angel armed with a flaming sword, who will let no one enter, now go, leave, I never want to see you again. Bearing on their backs the stinking animal hides, staggering along on unsteady legs, adam and eve resembled two orang-utans who had stood upright for the first time. Outside of the garden of eden, the earth was arid and inhospitable, the lord was not exaggerating when he threatened adam with thorns and thistles. As he had so rightly said, the good life was over.

2

Their first home was a low, narrow cave, well, it was more of a cavity than a cave, which they discovered in a rocky outcrop to the north of the garden of eden when they were searching desperately for some shelter. There, at last, they could take refuge from the brutal, burning sun that bore no resemblance to the invariably benign temperatures to which they were accustomed and that had remained constant day and night and at any season of the year. They abandoned the heavy skins that were suffocating them with their heat and stench and returned to their initial nakedness, although to protect the more delicate parts of the body, those that are only partially shielded by the thighs, they resorted to using thinner skins with shorter hair and invented what would later come to be called a skirt, identical in form for women and for men. They went hungry for the first few days, with not even a crust of bread to chew on. The garden of eden was full of fruit, indeed, that was all there was to eat, and even those animals, who should, given their nature as carnivores, feed on red meat, even they, by divine command, had to submit to the same melancholy, unsatisfactory diet. What we don't know is where those skins came from that the lord had summoned up with a snap of his fingers, like a magician. They clearly came from animals, and large ones too, but who had killed and skinned them and where, no one knows. By chance, there was some water nearby, but it was only a somewhat muddy stream and was nothing like the wide river that had its source in the garden of eden and then divided into four, with one branch irrigating the region reputed to have an abundance of gold and with the other flowing through the land of cush. And strange though this may seem to today's readers, the remaining two branches were immediately baptised with the names tigris and euphrates. Faced by the humble little stream laboriously threading its way through the thorns and thistles of the desert, it seems likely that the river had merely been an optical illusion created by the lord himself to make life in the earthly paradise more pleasant. Anything is possible. Yes, anything is possible, even eve's extraordinary idea of going to ask the angel for permission to enter the garden of eden and pick some fruit to keep them alive for a few more days. Adam was as sceptical as any man is regarding the success of any enterprise born of a woman's brain and so he told her to go alone and to prepare to be disappointed, That angel over there, guarding the gate with his flaming sword, is not just any angel, with no weight or authority, he's one of the cherubim, so do you really expect him to disobey the lord's orders, he asked very sensibly, That I don't know nor will I until I try, And if you fail, If I fail, I will have lost only the steps I took from there to here and the words I said to him, she replied, Yes, but we'll be in deep trouble if the angel goes and denounces us to the lord, What, more trouble than we're in already, with no way of earning our living, with no food, no roof over our heads and no clothes worthy of the name, how much more trouble could we be in, the lord has already punished us by expelling us from the garden of eden, and I can't imagine anything worse than that, We have no way of knowing what the lord can or cannot do, In that case, we should demand that he explain himself, and the first thing he should tell us is why he did what he did and to what purpose, You're mad, Better mad than fainthearted, Don't you be disrespectful to me, shouted adam angrily, besides, I'm not fainthearted and I'm not afraid, Well, neither am I, so that makes us even, and there's nothing more to be said, Fine, but don't you forget that I'm the one who gives the orders around here, So the lord said, agreed eve with the look of someone who has uttered not a word. When the sun had lost some of its strength, she set off wearing her skirt and with one of the lighter skins draped over her shoulders. She looked, you might say, very proper, although she could do nothing about her bare breasts, which bobbed about as she walked. She couldn't help it, nor did she even give it a thought, after all, there was no one around to be attracted by them, and, at the time, breasts served only for suckling and little more. She was surprised at herself, at how freely and fearlessly she had replied to her husband, without having to choose her words, merely saying what, in her view, the case merited. It was as if there were another woman inside her, quite independent of the lord and of the husband he had given her, a woman, in short, who had decided to make full use of the tongue and the language that the lord had, in a manner of speaking, stuck down her throat. She crossed the stream, enjoying the coolness of the water that seemed to spread through her veins and simultaneously experiencing something that might have been happiness, well, something, at least, that bore a close resemblance to that word. Then she felt a pang of hunger, this was hardly the moment for such positive thoughts. She waded out of the stream and picked a few sour berries which, although they weren't exactly nourishing, did for a while, a very short while, assuage the need to eat. The garden of eden is very close now, you can clearly see the tops of the tallest trees. Eve is walking more slowly than before and not because she's feeling tired. If adam were here, he would laugh at her, Where's all your bravery now, you're really scared. Yes, she was scared, scared of failing, scared that she wouldn't find the right words to persuade the guard, in fact, she felt so discouraged that she found herself muttering, It would be much easier if I were a man. There is the angel, and in his right hand, the flaming sword shines with a malevolent light. Eve tried to cover her breasts and then went over to him. What do you want, asked the angel, I'm hungry, said the woman, There's nothing here for you to eat, But I'm hungry, she insisted, You and your husband were driven out of the garden of eden by the lord and there is no appeal against that sentence, go away, Would you kill me if I tried to go in, asked eve, That's why I was placed here on guard, You didn't answer my question, Those are my orders, To kill me, Yes, And would you obey that order. The angel did not respond. He merely moved his arm, and the flaming sword in his hand hissed like a serpent. That was his reply. Eve took a step nearer. Stop, said the angel, You'll have to kill me, then, because I won't stop, and she took another step, you'll be left guarding an orchard of rotten fruit that no one will want to eat, god's orchard, the lord's orchard, she added. What do you want, asked the angel again, apparently unaware that repeating the question would be interpreted as a sign of weakness, As I said, I'm hungry, Well, I assumed you'd both be far away by now, Where would we go, asked eve, we're in the middle of a strange desert with not a single path or road, where we haven't seen another living soul all the time we've been here, we sleep in a hole, we eat grass, just as the lord promised, and we have diarrhoea, What's diarrhoea, asked the angel, Another word for it is the runs, the vocabulary the lord taught us has a word for everything, having diarrhoea or the runs, if you prefer that term, means that you can't retain the shit you have inside you, What does that mean, Ah, that's the advantage of being an angel, said eve, and smiled. The angel liked that smile. In heaven, people smiled a lot too, but always seraphically and with the slightly embarrassed look of someone apologising for being so contented, if you could call it contentment. Eve had won the dialectic battle, now she just had to win the battle for food. The angel said, All right, I'll bring you some fruit, but don't tell anyone, My lips are sealed, although my husband will have to know, Come back here with him tomorrow, we need to talk. Eve removed the skin from around her shoulders and said, Use this to carry the fruit in. She was naked from the waist up. The sword hissed more loudly as if it had received a sudden influx of energy, the same energy that led the angel to take a step forward, the same that made him raise his left hand and touch the woman's breast. Nothing else happened, nothing else could happen, angels, as long as they are angels, are forbidden any carnal commerce, only fallen angels were free to get together with whoever they wanted or whoever wanted them. Eve smiled and placed her hand on the angel's hand and pressed it gently to her breast. Her body was grimy, her nails were as black as if she had been using them to dig the earth, her hair was like a tangled nest of eels, but she was a woman, the only one. The angel had gone into the garden, where he took his time picking the most nutritious and luscious of fruits, before returning laden down with a goodly burden. Here you are, he said, and eve asked, What's your name, and he replied, My name is azael, Thank you for the fruit, azael, Well, I could hardly let the creatures whom the lord created starve, The lord will be grateful to you, but it's best you don't tell him about this. The angel either appeared not to hear or really didn't hear, occupied as he was in helping eve put the bulging load on her back, meanwhile saying, Come back tomorrow with adam, there are a few things you need to know, We'll be here, she said.

The following day, adam went with his wife to the garden of eden. At her suggestion, they had washed themselves as best they could in the stream, although their best was very little, almost nothing really, because without the aid of soap,

16

water can give only an illusion of cleanliness. They sat down on the ground and discovered that the angel azael wasn't one to beat about the bush, You are not the only human beings on earth, he began, Not the only ones, exclaimed adam, astonished, Please, don't make me repeat myself, Who created those other beings, where are they, They're everywhere, Did the lord create them as he created us, asked eve, That I can't say, and if you ask the same question again, our conversation will end right here, and we will each go our separate ways, I to my job of guarding the garden of eden and you to your cave and your hunger, In that case, we'll be dead in no time, said adam, no one has ever taught me how to do anything, I can't dig or work the land because I have no hoe and no plough, and if I had, I would have to learn how to use them and there's no one in this desert to teach me, we would be better off as the dust we came from, with no will and no desire, You speak like a book, said the angel, and adam felt pleased to have spoken like a book, he who had never studied. Then eve asked, If other human beings already exist, why did the lord make us, As you know, the ways of the lord are mysterious, but, as far as I can make out, you were an experiment, Us, an experiment, exclaimed adam, an experiment to prove what, Since I do not know for certain, I cannot tell you, but the lord must have his reasons for keeping silent on the matter, We aren't a matter, we are two people who don't know how we're going to survive, said eve, Wait, I haven't yet finished, said the angel, Speak then, and please give us some scrap of good news, however insignificant, Not far from here is a road occasionally frequented by caravans of traders travelling back and forth to the markets, and my idea is that you should light a fire that produces a lot of smoke, enough to be seen from a distance, We haven't anything to light it with, said eve, You don't, but I do, What, This burning sword, which will finally be of some use, I just need to apply the tip to some dry thistles and some straw and you'll have a bonfire that can be seen not just by a passing caravan, but even from the moon itself, although you must take care not to let the fire spread, because a bonfire is one thing and a whole desert in flames quite another, it might reach the garden of eden, and then I'd be out of a job, And what if no one comes, asked eve, Oh, they will, they will, don't you worry about that, replied azael, human beings are naturally curious, they'll want to know who lit that fire and why, And then, asked adam, Then it's up to you, I can't do anything more, you simply have to find a way of joining the caravan, just tell them that you'll work for your keep, I'm sure that two pairs of hands in exchange for a dish of lentils would be a good deal for all concerned, both for employer and employee, but when that happens, don't forget to put out the fire, that way I'll know you've gone, and that, adam, will be your chance to learn all the things you don't know. It was an excellent plan, some cherubim are a real boon, and whereas the lord, at least as regards this experiment, cared nothing about the future of his two creations, azael, the angelic guard charged with keeping them out of the garden of eden, welcomed them in christian fashion, gave them food and, above all, equipped them for life with a few precious practical ideas, a true road to salvation for the body and, therefore, the soul. The couple could not thank him enough, eve even shed a few tears when she embraced azael, a display of affection that greatly displeased her husband, and later on, he couldn't help but ask the question that was bursting to be asked, Did you give him something in exchange, What and to whom, asked eve, knowing full well what her husband meant, Who do you think, to him, azael, said adam, carefully omitting the first part of the question, He's an angel, one of the cherubim, replied eve, and felt it unnecessary to say anything more. Some say that this was the day on which the battle of the sexes really began. The first caravan of traders did not appear for three weeks. Rather than them all trudging up to the cave where adam and eve were living, they sent an advance guard of three men who had the authority to negotiate any work contracts, they, however, took pity on the luckless pair and made room for them on the donkeys they were riding. The leader of the caravan would decide what to do with them. Despite this uncertainty, adam, like someone closing a door as he says goodbye, put out the fire. When the last wisp of smoke had disappeared into the atmosphere, the angel said, Ah, they've gone, safe journey.

3

Life treated them fairly well. They were accepted into the caravan despite their evident lack of labouring skills and were not required to give too many explanations about who they were and where they came from. They had got lost, they said, and that, after all, was the truth of the matter. Apart from the fact that they were the children of the lord, the work of his own divine hands, something which no one there could possibly know, there were no obvious physiognomic differences between them and their providential hosts, you would even think they belonged to the same race, black hair, olive skin, dark eyes, striking eyebrows. When cain is born, all the neighbours will be surprised by the pale rosy complexion with which he comes into the world, as if he were the son of an angel, or an archangel, or even, perish the thought, the son of one of the cherubim. They never lacked for a dish of lentils, and it was not long before adam and eve began to earn a wage, nothing much, a purely symbolic amount really, but it nevertheless represented a start in life. Not only adam, but eve as well, who had not been born to be a duchess, were gradually being initiated into the mysteries of manual labour, into operations as simple as making a slip knot in a rope or as complex as handling a needle without pricking your fingers too often. When the caravan arrived at the settlement from which it had set out some weeks before, adam and eve were given a tent and some mats to sleep on and it was thanks to that and to other periods of stability in their lives that adam could, at last, learn to dig and delve, to sow seed in a furrow, and even to perfect the sublime art of pruning, which no lord and no god had thought to invent. He began to work with the tools that others lent him, then slowly acquired his own and, after only a few years, was considered by his neighbours to be a good farmer. The days spent in the garden of eden and in the cave in the desert, the days of thorns and thistles and muddy streams, faded from his memory until sometimes they seemed like gratuitous inventions that had never actually been experienced or even dreamed, but, rather, intuited as if they came from a life, a self, a destiny that might have been. Eve, it is true, kept a special place in her memory for azael, the angel who had disobeyed the lord's instructions in order to save his creations from death, but that was their secret, vouchsafed to no one else. Then came the day when adam could buy a piece of land, call it his own and build, at the foot of a hill, a rough adobe house, and there his three sons were born, cain, abel and seth, all of whom, at some point in their lives, crawled between kitchen and living room. And between the kitchen and the fields as well, because the two oldest boys, as soon as they were big enough, and with all the ingenuous guile of their few years, used every pretext, valid or not, to get their father to take them with him, mounted on the family mule, to wherever he was working. It became clear early on that they had very different vocations. While abel preferred the company of sheep and lambs, cain's great joy lay in hoes and pitchforks and scythes, one was clearly destined to make his way raising livestock, the other to forge a path in agriculture. It has to be said that the division of labour in the household could not have been better, given than it covered the two most important sectors of the economy at the time. Everyone agreed that it was a family with a future. And so it would prove, as would shortly be shown, with the invaluable help of the lord, of course, for that is what he is there for. Ever since they were but tender infants, cain and abel had been the best of friends, to the degree that they did not even seem like brothers, where one went, the other followed, and they did everything by mutual agreement. Those the lord loves, he preserves, said jealous mothers in the village, and so it seemed. Then one day, the future decided that it was about time it put in an appearance. Abel had his livestock, cain his fields, and in accordance with tradition and religious obligation, they offered to the lord the first fruits of their labours, with abel burning the delicate flesh of a lamb and cain the products of the earth, a few ears of wheat and some seeds. Then something happened that has still not been explained. The smoke from the meat offered by abel rose straight up and vanished into infinite space, a sign that the lord accepted the sacrifice and was well pleased, but the smoke from cain's vegetables, nurtured with just as much love, hardly rose up at all and dispersed when it was barely a few feet above the ground, which meant that the lord had rejected it out of hand. Concerned and perplexed, cain suggested to abel that they change places, perhaps it was the wind causing the problem, but when they did change places, the result was the same. It was clear that the lord held cain in contempt. It was then that abel revealed his true nature. Instead of feeling for his brother in his misfortune and consoling him, he mocked him and, as if that were not enough, began to put on airs, proclaiming himself, to cain's astonishment and bafflement, to be the lord's favourite, the lord's chosen one. Poor cain had no alternative but to swallow the insult and go back to work. The same scene was repeated unvaryingly over a whole week, with one plume of smoke rising up to the heavens and one rising only as high as a man could reach before it dispersed. And abel always reacted with the same lack of compassion, the same disdainful remarks, the same scorn. One day, cain asked his brother to go with him to a nearby valley where it was said that a fox had its lair, and there, with his own hands, he slew him with the jaw-bone of an ass that he had previously hidden, with treacherous intent, in a bramble patch. At that very moment, that is, after the event, the voice of the lord rang out, indeed, he appeared to cain in person. Not a word for years and suddenly there he was, dressed as he had been when he drove the two brothers' unfortunate parents from the garden of eden. He was clothed from head to foot in a richly woven robe, on his head the triple crown and in his right hand the sceptre. Where is your brother, he asked, and cain responded with another question. Am I my brother's keeper, You killed him, Yes, I did, but you are the one who is really to blame, I would have given my life for him if you had not destroyed mine, It was a question of putting you to the test, But why put to the test the very thing you yourself created, Because I am the sovereign lord of all things, And of all beings you will say, but not of me and my freedom, What, the freedom to kill, Just as you had the freedom to stop me killing abel, which was perfectly within your capabilities, all you had to do, just for a moment, was to abandon that pride in your infallibility that you share with all the other gods, and, again just for a moment, to be truly merciful and accept my offering with humility, because you shouldn't have refused it, you gods, you and all the others, have a duty to those you claim to have created, This is seditious talk, Yes, possibly, but I can guarantee you that if I were god, I would repeat every day Blessed are those who choose sedition because theirs is the kingdom of the earth, That's sacrilege, Maybe, but no more sacrilegious than you allowing abel to die, You were the one who killed him, True, but you were the one who pronounced sentence, whereas I merely carried out the execution, That blood over there wasn't spilled by me, you could have chosen between good and evil, but you chose evil and must pay for it, The person who stays to keep watch over the guard is just as much a thief as the one who actually goes into the vineyard, said cain, That blood is crying out for vengeance, insisted god, In that case, you will have your revenge both for a real death and for another that did not take place, Explain yourself, You won't like what you hear, Don't worry about that, speak, It's simple enough, I killed abel because I couldn't kill you, so, in intent, you are dead too, Yes, I see what you mean, but death is forbidden for the gods, Oh, I know, but you gods should still take the blame for all the crimes committed in your name or because of you, God is innocent, it would be just the same if I didn't exist, But because I killed someone, I could now be slain by anyone who meets me, No, I'll make an agreement with you, God make an agreement with a reprobate, asked cain, unable to believe what he was hearing, Let's say it's an agreement based on our shared responsibility for abel's death, So you recognise your share in the blame, Yes, I do, but don't tell anyone, it will be a secret between god and cain, This can't be true, I must be dreaming, That often happens with gods, Is that because your ways are, as they say, mysterious, asked cain, No god I know ever said such a thing, it would never even occur to us that our ways are mysterious, no, that was something invented by men who presume to know god intimately, So I won't be punished for my crime then, asked cain, My portion of the blame does not absolve yours, you will have your punishment, Which is, You will be a fugitive and a vagabond upon the earth, In that case, anyone will have the right to kill me, No, because I will put a mark upon your forehead, and no one will harm you, but to repay me for my benevolence, you must try to do no harm to anyone else, said the lord, and with the tip of his index finger he touched cain's forehead on which there appeared a small black mark, That is the mark of your condemnation, added the lord, but it is also a sign that for the whole of your life you will be subject to my protection and to my censure too,

I will be watching you wherever you are, All right, I accept, said cain, You have no option, When does my punishment begin, Now, May I say goodbye to my parents, asked cain, That's up to you, I don't involve myself in family matters, but they will certainly want to know where abel is and I don't imagine you're going to tell them you killed him, No, No what, No, I won't say goodbye to my parents, Off you go, then. There was nothing more to be said. The lord disappeared before cain had even taken his first step. Abel's face was covered in flies, there were flies on his open eyes, flies in the corners of his mouth, flies on the wounds on his hands which he had held up to protect himself from the blows. Poor abel, deceived by god. The lord had made some very bad choices when it came to inaugurating the garden of eden, in this particular game of roulette everyone had lost, in this target practice for the blind no one had scored. Of course, eve and adam could always have another child to make up for the loss of their murdered son, but how sad to be someone with no other goal in life than to keep making children without knowing why or for what purpose. In order to propagate the species, say those who believe in a final objective, in an ultimate reason, although they have no idea what those might be and have never bothered to ask themselves why the species should keep being propagated as if it were the universe's one last hope. Cain has already given his answer by killing abel because he could not kill the lord. Things do not augur well for the future life of this man.

4

And yet this harried man setting off, pursued by his own footsteps, this wretch, this fratricide, had more principles than most. Just ask his mother, who would often find him sitting on the damp ground in their vegetable patch, staring at a small, newly planted tree, waiting for it to grow. He was four or five years old and he wanted to see trees grow. Then she, apparently even more imaginative than her son, explained to him that trees are very shy and only grow when no one is looking at them, They're embarrassed, you see, she said to him one day. For a few moments, cain said nothing, but after some thought, replied, Then don't look at them, mama, they're not shy with me, they're used to me. Sensing what would happen next, his mother looked away, and immediately her son's voice rang out triumphantly, It grew, it grew, you see, I told you not to look. That night, when adam returned from work, eve, laughing, told him what had happened, and her husband replied, That boy will go far. And perhaps he would have done if the lord had not crossed his path. And yet, he has already gone quite far, although not in the sense that his father had meant. Dragging weary feet, he was now tramping through a desolate landscape without so much as a ruined shack in sight or any other sign of life, a terrifying wilderness made more menacing still by the blank sky and the threat of an imminent downpour. There was no shelter anywhere, apart from under one of the few trees, which, as he walked, were beginning to show their tops above the horizon. The branches, usually only sparsely covered with leaves, did not guarantee any protection worthy of the name. It was then, as the first drops fell, that cain realised that his tunic was stained with blood. He thought perhaps the rain would wash it away, but then thought better of it and tried to disguise the stain with earth, no one would ever suspect what lay beneath, especially since there was no shortage in such places of people with grubby, grimy tunics. It began to rain hard, and his tunic was soon soaked, and not a trace of blood was left, besides, if asked, he could always say it was lamb's blood. Yes, he said out loud, but abel was no lamb, he was my brother, and I killed him. At that precise moment, he forgot what he had said to the lord about them both being guilty of the murder, but his memory soon came to his aid, which is why he added, If it's true what they say, that the lord knows all and can do all, then he could have removed that jaw-bone and then I wouldn't have killed abel and we could be standing together at the door of our house watching the rain, and abel would agree that the lord had been quite wrong not to accept the only things I had to offer in sacrifice, the seeds and the ears of wheat born of my hard work and the sweat of my brow, and he would still be alive and we would be the same firm friends we always were. Crying over spilt milk is not as pointless as people say, it is in a way instructive because it shows the true scale of the frivolity of certain human behaviour, because if milk is spilled, it's spilled and all you can do is clean it up, and if abel died a cruel death that's because someone took his life. Thinking while getting soaked to the skin is not the most comfortable thing in the world and that is perhaps why, from one moment to the next, the rain stopped, so that cain could think at his leisure and freely follow the course of his thoughts until he found out where they would lead him. Neither he nor we will ever know, for the sudden appearance, out of nowhere, of a dilapidated hut distracted him from his ponderings and from his griefs. There were signs that the land behind the house had once been worked, the inhabitants had clearly long ago abandoned it, although perhaps not so very long ago if we bear in mind the intrinsic fragility, the precarious cohesion of the materials used to build such humble dwellings, which require constant repairs if they are not to collapse in a single season. With no careful hand to watch over it, such a house will have little chance of withstanding the corrosive effect of the elements, especially the drenching rain and the rough winds that rasp away at it like sandpaper. Some of the interior walls had crumbled, most of the roof had fallen in, and all that remained was a relatively sheltered corner where the exhausted traveller could collapse. He could barely stand, not just because of the distance he had walked, but also because hunger was beginning to bite. Evening was coming on, soon it would be night. I'm going to stay here, said cain out loud, as was his custom whenever he needed to calm himself, even though he was not under threat from anyone just then, indeed, it was unlikely that even the lord himself knew where he was. It isn't particularly cold, but his wet tunic, clinging to his skin, is making him shiver. He reckons that by taking it off he would kill two birds with one stone, firstly, because then he would stop feeling cold and, secondly, because the tunic, being made of fairly thin fabric, would soon dry. And so he took off the tunic and immediately felt better. True, it didn't seem quite right to be sitting there as naked as the day he was born, but he was alone, there were no witnesses, no one who could touch him. This thought provoked another shiver, although not of the same sort, not of the kind he had felt from contact with his wet tunic, but a kind of tremor in the genital region, a slight stiffening that quickly went away, as if ashamed of itself. Cain knew what this was, but, despite his youth, either paid it little heed or else feared that more evil than good would come of it. He curled up in his corner, knees to chest, and fell asleep. The cold of dawn woke him. He reached out to touch the tunic, noticed that it was still a little damp, but decided to put it on anyway and let it dry on his body. He had had no dreams or nightmares, he had slept as one imagines a stone must sleep, without consciousness, without responsibility, without guilt, however, his first words when he woke were, I killed my brother. In a different age, he might perhaps have wept, he might perhaps have despaired, he might perhaps have beaten his chest or his head, but things being what they are, with the world so recently begun, we still lack many of the words with which we can begin to try to say who we are and cannot always find those that will best explain it, and so he contented himself with repeating what he had said until the words ceased to mean anything and were just a series of incoherent sounds, meaningless babblings. He realised then that he had, in fact, had a dream, well, not a dream exactly, but an image of himself returning home and finding his brother standing in the doorway, waiting for him. That is how he will remember him for the rest of his life, as if he had made peace with his crime and had no further need for his feelings of remorse.

He left the hut and took a deep breath of cold air. The sun had not yet risen, but the sky was lit with delicate colours, enough for the arid, monotonous landscape before him to appear transfigured in that early morning light, a kind of garden of eden with no prohibitions. Cain had no reason to set off in any particular direction, but he instinctively sought the footsteps he had left behind him before he had departed from his route to investigate the hut where he had spent the night. It was simple enough, he just had to walk towards the sun, which would soon be appearing above the horizon. Apparently soothed by those hours of sleep, his stomach had moderated its pangs and would, with luck, remain in the same quiet mood because there was no hope of finding any food soon, and although it's true that he did come across the occasional fig tree, there was never any fruit, it not being the season. With a remnant of energy he didn't even know he had, he set off once more. The sun came up, it won't rain today, and it might even be hot. It wasn't long before he began to feel tired again. He had to find something to eat, if not, he would die in that desert and, within a matter of days, be nothing but a skeleton, because the carnivorous birds or the occasional pack of wild dogs that had not as yet appeared would make short work of him. It was written, however, that cain's life would not end there, mainly because it would not have been worth the lord's while to have spent so much time cursing him only to leave him to die in that wasteland. The news came from below, from his weary feet, which had taken a while to realise that the ground they were walking on had changed, there was now no vegetation, no scrub or thistles to hinder his steps, in short, cain, without knowing how or when, had found a path. The poor wanderer was thrilled because it is a well-known fact that a road, path or track will lead sooner or later, nearer or farther, to an inhabited place where it might be possible to find work, a roof and a crust of bread to assuage his hunger. Encouraged by this sudden discovery, and, as they say, putting a good face on a bad business, he dredged up some energy from nowhere and quickened his pace, expecting at any moment to see a house, signs of life, a man mounted on a donkey or a woman carrying a pitcher on her head. He still had to walk a long way though. The old man who finally appeared was on foot and leading two sheep along on a rope. Cain greeted him as warmly as his vocabulary allowed, but the man did not reciprocate. What's that mark on your forehead, he asked. Taken by surprise, cain asked in turn, What mark, That one, said the man, raising his hand to his own head, It's a birthmark, replied

32

cain, You're obviously not a good man, Who told you, how do you know, answered cain unwisely, As the old saying goes, the devil marks those he finds fault with, Oh, I'm no better or worse than anyone else, I'm just looking for work, said cain, trying to lead the conversation in the direction that best suited him, There's no shortage of work around here, what can you do, asked the old man, I'm a farmer, We've got enough farmers, you won't find any of that kind of work, besides, you're on your own, no family, No, I lost mine, How, I just lost them, that's all, In that case, I'll leave you, I don't like the look of you or that mark on your forehead. He was about to move off when cain stopped him, Don't go, at least tell me the name of this place, They call it the land of nod, And what does nod mean, It means the land of fugitives or wanderers, and seeing as how you're here, tell me, what are you fleeing from and why are you a wanderer, Look, I'm not going to tell my life story to someone I happen to meet on the road, a man leading two sheep along by a rope, besides, I don't know you, I owe you no particular respect and am under no obligation to answer your questions, We'll meet again, Who knows, I might not find work here and have to move on, If you can make adobe bricks and build a wall, this is the place for you, Where should I go, then, asked cain, Take the next road on the right, at the bottom is a square, and there you'll find your answer, Goodbye, old man, Goodbye, and may you never be old yourself, What do you mean by that, That the mark on your forehead is no birthmark, that you didn't put it there yourself, and that nothing you have told me is true,

33

Perhaps my truth is your lie, Perhaps, but doubt is the privilege of those who have lived a long time, that's why you couldn't persuade me to accept as truths what seemed to me more like falsehoods, Who are you, asked cain, Careful, lad, if you ask me who I am, you'll be acknowledging my right to ask you who you are, Nothing will force me to tell you that, You're about to enter this city, you're going to stay here, sooner or later everything will be known, Only if there's no other way and certainly not from my lips, At least tell me your name, My name is abel, said cain.

While the false abel is walking towards the square where, according to the old man, his destiny awaits him, let us attend to the extremely pertinent observation made by a few of our more vigilant and attentive readers, who consider that the dialogue we have just set down would be historic- ally and culturally impossible, that a farmer with little and now no land and an old man with no apparent means of support would never think or speak like that. They are quite right, of course, however, it's not so much a question of them having or not having the ideas and the necessary vocabu- lary to express those ideas, but of our own capacity to accept, even if only out of simple human empathy and intellectual generosity, that a peasant from the very earliest times and an old man leading two sheep along by a piece of rope, with only a limited knowledge and a language that is still only taking its first tentative steps, were driven by the need to try out ways of expressing premonitions and intuitions appar- ently beyond their reach. Obviously, they didn't say those actual words, but the doubts, suspicions, perplexities, argumentative advances and retreats were nevertheless there. All we did was put into a modern idiom the twofold and, for us, insoluble mystery of the language and thought of the time. If the result is coherent now, it would have been then, given that we're all of us muleteers travelling down the same road. All of us, both the learned and the ignorant.

There is the square. Calling this place a city was something of an exaggeration. A few higgledy-piggledy earth-built houses, a few children playing some game or other, a few adults moving about like sleepwalkers, a few donkeys that seem to go wherever they wish and not where they're supposed to, no city worthy of the name would recognise itself in the primitive scene before us now, there are no cars or buses, no road signs, no traffic lights, no underpasses, no billboards on the frontages or the roofs of houses, in a word, no modernity, no modern life. They'll get there though, progress, as it will come to be known later on, is inevitable, as inevitable as death. And as life. At the far end of the square, a building is under construction, a kind of rustic two-storey palace, although nothing to compare with the likes of mafra or versailles or buckingham palace, on which dozens of bricklayers and their assistants are labouring, the latter carrying adobe bricks on their backs, the former laying them out in regular lines. Cain knows nothing about building work, advanced or otherwise, but his destiny is waiting for him here, however bitter it may turn out to be, but that's something you only know when it's too late to change and you have no option but to confront it. Like a man. Doing his best to disguise his nervousness and the hunger that was

35

making his legs tremble, he went over to the building site. At first, the workmen, who didn't know him, assumed he was one of those idle individuals who, throughout the ages, have enjoyed watching other people work, but they were quick to realise that he was simply another victim of the crisis, a poor man in search of work and salvation. Almost without cain having to say why he was there, they directed him to the overseer in charge, Talk to him, they said. Cain did as they advised, climbed up to the observer's perch and, after exchanging the usual greetings, explained that he was looking for work. The overseer asked, What can you do, and cain answered, I'm a farmer by trade, but I imagine you could always use an extra pair of hands, Not a pair of hands, no, given that you know nothing about laying bricks, but a pair of feet perhaps, Feet, asked cain, uncomprehending, Yes, a pair of feet to tread the mud, Ah, Wait here, I'll talk to the clerk of works. He was already walking away when he turned his head to ask, What's your name, Abel, answered cain. The overseer was not gone long, You can start work right away, I'll take you to the treading pit, How much will I earn, asked cain, The treaders all earn the same, Yes, but how much, That's not my business, besides, if you want my advice, don't ask, they don't like it, first you have to show what you're worth, in fact, don't ask anything, just wait until they pay you, Well, if you think that's wisest, I'll do as you say, but it doesn't seem fair, It's best not to be impatient here, Who does the city belong to, what's their name, asked cain, What, the name of the city or its owner, Both, The city doesn't yet have a name, some call it one thing and others

36

another, but this area is known as the land of nod, Yes, an old man I met when I arrived told me, Was he an old man leading two sheep by a piece of rope, asked the overseer, Yes, He turns up now and then, but he doesn't live around here, And the owner, who's that, The owner is a woman, and her name is lilith, Doesn't she have a husband, asked cain, Well, I've heard tell his name is noah, but she's in charge of the flock, said the overseer, and then announced, Here's the treading pit. A group of men with their tunics tied in a knot above their knees were trudging round and round on a thick layer of mud, straw and sand, determinedly trampling it down, in the absence of any machine, to make it as homogeneous as possible. It wasn't a job that required much knowledge, just a pair of good, solid legs, and, if possible, a full stomach, which, as we know, was not the case with cain. The overseer said, In you go and just do what the others do, Look, I haven't eaten for three days, and I'm afraid my strength might give out and I'd end up in the mud, said cain, Come with me, But I haven't any money, You can pay later, come with me. They went over to a kind of kiosk on one side of the square, where they sold food. Not wishing to overload the story with unnecessary historical detail, we will not describe the modest menu, whose ingredients, at least in some cases, we would be unable to identify. The food seemed tasty enough, though, and cain tucked into it with a will. Then the overseer asked, What's that mark on your forehead, it doesn't look natural, It may not look natural, but it is, I was born with it, It's as if someone had put it there, That's what the old man with the two sheep said as well, but he was wrong, as are you, If you say so, Yes, I do and I'll repeat it as often as I have to, but I would prefer to be left in peace, after all, if, instead of this mark, I was lame, you wouldn't keep pointing it out to me, You're right, I won't bother you again, You're not bothering me, indeed, I should thank you for all your help, for the job, for this food, which is rapidly setting body and soul to rights, and perhaps for one thing more, What's that, Somewhere to sleep, Oh, that's easy enough, I can get you a mat and there's an inn over there, I'll talk to the owner, You really are a good samaritan, said cain, A samaritan, asked the overseer, intrigued, what's that, You know, I'm not sure, the word just came out, I don't know what it means either, You obviously have more things in your head than one would think to look at you, You mean this filthy tunic, Don't worry, I'll give you a clean one of mine, you can use the one you're wearing to work in, From what I know of the world, there can't be many good men in it and yet I've been lucky enough to meet one of them, Have you finished, asked the overseer somewhat abruptly, as if he disliked compliments, Yes, I can't eat another mouthful, I don't remember ever having eaten so much, Now, to work. They returned to the palace, this time walking past the section that had been built before the wing that was currently under construction, and there, on a balcony, they saw a woman dressed in what must have been the height of fashion at the time, and that woman, who, even from a distance, seemed very beautiful, was staring at them, as if she were looking straight through them, Who's that, asked cain, That's lilith, the owner of the palace and the city, just pray she doesn't take a fancy to you, Why, asked cain, There are stories going around, What stories, People say she's a witch and that she can drive a man crazy with her spells, What spells, asked cain, Don't ask, but I've seen a few men after they've had carnal commerce with her, And, They looked terrible, the poor wretches, like spectres, like ghosts of the men they were, You must be mad imagining a treader of mud ending up in bed with the queen of the city, You mean owner, Queen or owner, it's all the same, You obviously don't know much about women, they're capable of anything, of the best and the worst, they're as likely to scorn a crown and go down to the river to wash their lover's tunic as they are to trample on everything and everyone in order to get to sit on a throne, Are you speaking from experience, asked cain, From observation, that's all, that's why I'm the overseer, But you must have some experience, Yes, some, but I'm a bird with a very short wingspan, the sort that flies low, Well, I've never even flown once, You've never known a woman, asked the overseer, No, You've plenty of time, you're still young. Ahead of them lay the treading pit. The men were more or less lined up from the centre to the edge and now and then changed places, those on the inside moving to the outside and those on the outside moving to the inside. The overseer and cain waited for them to turn round and draw alongside them. Then the overseer tapped cain on the shoulder and said, Enter.

Like everything else, words have their whys and wherefores. Some call to us solemnly, arrogantly, giving themselves airs, as if they were destined for great things, and then it turns out that they were nothing more than a breeze too light even to set the sail of a windmill moving, whereas other ordinary, habitual words, the sort you use every day, end up having consequences no one would have dared predict, they weren't born for that and yet they shook the world. The overseer said, Enter, and it was as if he were saying, In you go and tread that mud and earn your daily bread, but weeks later, lilith will pronounce that very same word, letter for letter, when she summons the man whose name she has been told is abel, Enter. In a woman with a reputation for being very prompt when it came to satisfying her desires, it might seem strange that it had taken her weeks to open the door to her bedroom, but even this has an explanation, as will become clear. During that time, cain could not have imagined the ideas fermenting in the mind of that woman when she began visiting the treading pit, accompanied by an entourage of guards, slaves and other servants. She was like one of those jolly landowners who goes to the harvest to see for himself how hard his people are working, hoping to encourage them with his visit and offering a cheery word and even a comradely joke which, whether intentionally or not, will make everyone laugh. Lilith, however, didn't speak, or, rather, only to the overseer, whom she questioned about how work was progressing and asked repeatedly, seemingly just to make conversation, where the various workmen came from, those not originally from the city, that one over there, for example, I don't know, madam, when I asked him, because if you don't ask you don't know who you're dealing with, he just pointed over towards the west and said three words, no more, What three words, He said, from over there, madam, Did he mention why he left his homeland, No, madam, And what is his name, Abel, madam, he told me his name was abel, Is he a good worker, Yes, madam, he's the sort who talks little and works hard, And what's that mark on his forehead, Oh, I asked him that too and he says it's a birthmark, So we know nothing about this man called abel who came from the west, He's not the only one, madam, apart from those men who come from around here and whom we more or less know, the others are all untold stories, wanderers, fugitives, and men of few words, they might open up to each other a bit, but I can't even be sure of that, And the man with the mark, how does he behave, In my opinion, he acts as if he wanted to go unnoticed, Well, I've noticed him, murmured lilith to herself. A few days later, a palace envoy came to the treading pit and asked cain if he had a skill. Cain replied that he had once been a farmer, but had had to leave his lands because of the bad harvests. The envoy took that information away with him and three days later returned with an order for the treader abel to present himself immediately at the palace. Cain followed the envoy just as he was, in his filthy old tunic now little more than a rag, and having cleaned off as much mud from his legs as he could. They entered the palace via a small side door that gave on to a hallway where two women were waiting. The envoy withdrew to report that abel, the treader of mud, had arrived and was in the care of the slave-women. Cain was led by them into a separate room, his clothes were removed and he was then washed with warm water from head to toe.

The insistent, probing touch of the women's hands provoked in him an erection he could do nothing to repress, always supposing such a thing is possible. They laughed and, in response, redoubled their efforts on his erect organ, which, amidst much laughter, they referred to as a silent flute, and which suddenly leapt from their hands, as supple as a snake. The result, given the circumstances, was all too predictable, the man suddenly ejaculated, in several spurts, which the slaves, kneeling down as they were, received on their faces and in their mouths. Cain experienced a sudden flash of insight, this was why they had come to fetch him from the treading pit, but not to give pleasure to mere slave-women, who must enjoy satisfactions more appropriate to their station. The overseer's prudent warning had gone unheeded, cain had walked straight into the trap towards which the owner of the palace had been gently, unhurriedly propelling him, as if unintentionally, as if distracted by a passing cloud and with her mind on other things. She had deliberately delayed delivering the final blow in order to allow time for the seed cast apparently at random on the ground to germinate and flower. As for the fruit, it was clear that he would not have to wait long to be picked. The slave-women appeared to be in no hurry and were concentrating now on extracting the last drops from cain's penis, which they took turns to raise greedily to their lips with the tip of one finger. Everything has an end, however, everything has its conclusion, a freshly washed tunic now covered the man's nakedness, and the hour, a most anachronistic word in this biblical story, has come for him to be led into the presence of the owner of the palace, who will tell him what is to be done with him. The envoy was waiting in the hallway, and one look was enough for him to guess what had gone on in that bathroom, not that he was shocked, well, in the course of their work, envoys see so many things that nothing can surprise them. Besides, people knew then as they do now that the flesh is supinely weak, which is not entirely its fault, for the spirit, whose duty, in principle, should be to raise a barrier against all temptations, is always the first to give in and wave the white flag of surrender. The envoy knew where he was taking the mud treader abel, where and why, but he didn't envy him, although he did envy him that lubricious episode with the slave-women, which had stirred his blood. This time, they entered the palace by the main door, because here nothing is done in secret, if lilith has found herself a new lover, then it's best that people should know about it right away, to avoid all the whispering and the rumours, all the giggles and the gossip, as would, of course, happen in other cultures and civilisations. The envoy said to a slave-woman waiting outside the antechamber, Go and tell your mistress that we're here. The slave duly went and returned with a message, Come with me, she said to cain, and then, to the envoy, You can go, you're not needed now. That's the way things are, never feel flattered at being entrusted with a delicate mission, for once the work is done, you will inevitably be told, You can go, you're not needed now, as envoys know all too well. Lilith was sitting on a carved wooden stool, she was wearing a robe that must have cost a fortune, a dress with a décolletage that revealed, with a minimum of modesty, the initial curve of her breasts, leaving the rest to the viewer's imagination. The slave-woman had withdrawn, they were alone. Lilith gave the man an appreciative look, appeared to like what she saw and said, You will be here in this antechamber, day and night, there is your bed and a bench to sit on, you will, until I decide otherwise, be my guard and allow no one, whoever they may be, to enter my room, apart from the slave-women who come to clean and tidy. Whoever they may be, madam, asked cain with apparent innocence, You have a quick mind, I see, if you're thinking of my husband, no, he is not authorised to enter either, but he knows that already, so there's no need for you to tell him, And what if he were to try to force his way in, You're a strong man, you'll be able to stop him, But I can't restrain with force someone who, being the lord of the city, is also lord of my life, You can if I order you to, Sooner or later I will have to pay for the consequences, Well, that, my young friend, is something no one in this world can avoid, but if you're a coward, if you feel unsure or afraid, the remedy is easy, you can go straight back to the mud, Well, I never considered treading mud to be my destiny, And I can't promise that you will always be a guard at lilith's bedroom door, It's enough that I am your guard for the moment, madam, Well said, you deserve a kiss for those words. Cain did not respond, he was listening to the voice of the overseer, Be careful, they say she's a witch, that she can drive a man mad with her spells. What are you thinking, asked lilith, Oh, nothing, madam, in your presence I am incapable of thought, I look at you and am amazed, Perhaps you deserve a second kiss, I am here, madam, But I am not, guard. She got up and smoothed her dress, slowly running her hands over her body, as if caressing, first, her breasts, then her belly, and finally her thighs, where her hands lingered, and while she did this she stared hard at the man, her face as expressionless as a statue's. The slave-women, free of moral constraints, had laughed in pure contentment, almost innocence, while they were amusing themselves manipulating the man's body, they had taken part in an erotic game of which they knew all the rules and regulations, whereas here, in this antechamber where no sound from outside can penetrate, lilith and cain are like two swordsmen sharpening their blades for a duel to the death. Lilith was no longer there, she had gone into her bedroom and closed the door, cain looked around him and his only refuge was the bench reserved for him. He sat down, suddenly frightened by what the next few days might hold. He felt like a prisoner, and she herself had said, You will be here day and night, although she had not added, You will, when I so decide, be my bull to cover me, a term that would seem not just vulgar but inappropriate, since covering is something that quadrupeds do, not human beings, but in a way it's very apt, because we human beings were quadrupeds once, and we know that what we now call arms and legs were, for a long time, only legs, until someone thought to say to those men-to-be, It's time you stood up. Cain is wondering if he shouldn't run away before it's too late, but what's the point, he knows perfectly well that he won't run away, inside that room is a woman who appears to enjoy giving him the brush-off, but who will one day say to him, Enter, and he will and in doing so, he will pass from one prison to another. I wasn't born for this, thinks cain. He wasn't born to kill his own brother, and yet he had left abel's corpse in the middle of the field with his eyes and mouth covered in flies, a fate for which abel had not been born either. Cain considers life and can find no explanation for it, there is that woman, who although clearly sick with desire, is enjoying postponing the moment of surrender, which is not at all the right word, because lilith, when she does finally open her legs to allow herself to be penetrated, will not be surrendering, but trying to devour the man to whom she said, Enter.

5

Cain has now done as ordered and slept in lilith's bed and, incredible though it may seem, it was precisely his lack of sexual experience that saved him from drowning in the vortex of lust that gripped the woman and, in an instant, made her explode into screams like one possessed. She ground her teeth, bit the pillow and then his shoulder, even drinking his blood. Cain laboured determinedly away on top of her, bewildered by her wild, brazen movements and cries, but, at the same time, another cain who was not him was observing the scene curiously, almost coldly, the flailing limbs, the bodily contortions, the postures that copulation itself demanded or imposed until the acme of orgasm was reached. The two lovers did not sleep much on that first night. Nor on the second or third or all the other nights that followed. Lilith was as insatiable as cain was inexhaustible, the interval between two erections and their respective ejaculations insignificant, almost non-existent, you might even say that they had both reached the future paradise of allah. On one such night, noah, the lord of the city and lilith's husband, entered the antechamber, having been informed by a trusted slave that something extraordinary was going on. This was not the first time he had done so. Noah was the most indulgent of husbands, and during all their so-called life in common, he had been incapable of getting his wife with child, and it was his awareness of this continual failure, and perhaps also the hope that lilith might end up becoming pregnant by one of her occasional lovers and finally give him a son he could call his heir, that had led him to adopt, almost without realising it, the attitude of conjugal permissiveness, which, over time, had become a comfortable modus vivendi, disturbed only by the very rare occasions on which lilith, moved by what we imagine must be that much-vaunted thing female compassion, decided to go to her husband's bedroom for a brief, unsatisfactory encounter that compromised neither of them, for he then felt under no obligation to demand more than he was given and she could not be accused of denying him his rights. Lilith, however, never allowed noah into her own bedroom. At that precise moment, and even though the door was closed, the vehemence of the two lovers' erotic enthusiasm was like a series of slaps in the poor man's face, giving rise to a feeling he had not experienced before, an intense hatred of the horseman currently mounting the mare lilith and making her whinny as never before. I'll kill him, noah said to himself, without considering the consequences of that action, for example, how lilith would react if her favourite lover was slain. I'll kill them both, thought noah, broadening out his plan, I'll kill him and her. These were mere dreams, fantasies, deliriums, noah will kill no one and he himself will have the good fortune to escape death without having to do a thing to avoid it. Not a sound emerges from the room now, but this does not mean that the corporeal party is over, the musicians are merely resting, and the orchestra will soon launch into the next dance, the one whose final violent paroxysm will be followed by exhaustion, at least until the following night. Noah has withdrawn, carrying with him his plan for vengeance, which he caresses as if he were stroking lilith's inaccessible body. We will see how it all ends.

Given what we have described, it's only natural that it will occur to someone to ask if cain isn't tired out, squeezed dry by his insatiable lover. He is tired out and squeezed dry, and as pale as death. His pallor is due simply to a lack of sunlight and exposure to the fresh air that makes plants flourish and people's skin turn brown. But anyone who had known this man before he entered lilith's bedroom, where his time is divided between the antechamber and sex, would be sure unknowingly to repeat the overseer's words, He's a ghost, a spectre, as the person chiefly responsible for his condition finally realised. You don't look well, she said, I'm fine, replied cain, Maybe, but your face says otherwise, It doesn't matter, Yes, it does, from now on you will go for a walk every day, you can take a slave with you so that no one bothers you, I want to see you with the face you had when I saw you at the treading pit, Your wish is my command, madam. The accompanying slave was chosen by lilith herself, what she didn't know, however, was that he was a double agent, who took his orders from noah, even though he was, for administrative purposes, her servant. Let us, therefore, fear the worst. On the first few occasions, the walks passed off without incident, the slave always walking one pace behind, listening attentively to whatever cain said and suggesting what he thought would be the best route to follow outside the city walls. There was no apparent reason for concern. Then, one day, concern arrived in the guise of three men waiting to ambush them and with whom, as cain quickly realised, the treacherous slave was in cahoots. What do you want, asked cain. The men did not answer. They were all armed, the apparent leader with a sword and the other two with knives. What do you want, cain asked again. The answer came in the form of a sword suddenly unsheathed and pointed at his chest, To kill you, said the man, stepping forward, Why, asked cain, Because your time is up, You can't kill me, said cain, the mark on my forehead will not allow you to, What mark, asked the man who was, it seems, somewhat shortsighted, This one here, said cain, Oh, yes, I can see it now, what I can't see is why a blemish would prevent me from killing you, It's not a blemish, it's a mark, And who put it there, did you do it yourself, asked the man, No, the lord put it there, What lord, The lord god. The man burst out laughing and the others, including the unfaithful slave, provided a gleeful chorus. Better the last smile than the first laugh, said cain, and then, addressing the gang's leader, Do you have family, he asked, Why do you want to know, Do you have children, a wife, a father and mother still alive, other relatives, Yes, but, You will not need to kill me for them to be punished, said cain, interrupting him, the sword in your hand has already condemned them, the lord's word on it,

50

Don't think you're going to lie your way out of this, shouted the man and advanced, sword at the ready. At that same moment, the weapon was transformed into a cobra which the man, horrified, shook from his hand, There, said cain, what you took for a snake was a sword. He bent down and picked the sword up by the hilt, I could kill you now, and no one would come to your aid, he said, your companions have fled, as will the traitor who brought me here, Forgive me, begged the man, kneeling down, Only the lord can forgive you, if he so chooses, I can't, now go, you will find the reward for your villainy at home. The man left, head down, weeping, tearing his hair, regretting a thousand times over ever having chosen the profession of murderous bandit. Repeating the steps he took when he first arrived, cain walked back into the city. Just as on that occasion, he turned a corner and found himself face to face with the old man leading the two sheep by a rope. Goodness, you've changed, said the old man, you don't look anything like the vagabond who came from the west or the treader of mud, No, I'm a guard now, said cain, and made as if to go on his way, Guarding which door, asked the old man in a tone that was intended to be mocking, but which sounded rather resentful, If you know already, why waste time asking, Because I don't know the details, and the savour of any story is always in the details, Well, go hang yourself on them then, you have a rope after all, retorted cain, and that way I wouldn't have to see you again. The old man shouted, You will go on seeing me until the end of your days, My days will have no end, answered cain, moving off, and watch that those sheep of yours don't eat the rope, That's what I'm here for, but it's all they think of doing.

Lilith was not in her room, nor on the roof terrace, where she often sunbathed naked. Sitting on his bench, cain considered the situation, trying to weigh up what had happened. It was clear that the slave had taken him down that path on purpose in order to meet the waiting bandits, so someone must have plotted against his life. It wasn't difficult to guess the name of what we would now call the mastermind behind that failed murder attempt. Noah, said cain, that's who it was, no one else in the palace or in the city would gain anything by my disappearance. At that moment, lilith came into the antechamber, That was a short walk, she said. A thin veil of sweat made the skin on her shoulders gleam, she was as succulent as a ripe pomegranate or as a split fig from which oozes the first honeyed drop. Cain considered carrying her off to bed, then abandoned the idea, perhaps later on, there were serious matters to deal with first. Someone tried to kill me, he said, Kill you, asked lilith, startled, who, The slave you sent with me and some hired bandits, What happened, tell me, The slave led me down a path out of the city, that's where the attack took place, Did they hurt you, wound you, No, How did you escape, asked lilith, No one can kill me, said cain calmly, You're the only person in the world who believes that, Yes, I am. There was a silence, which cain broke, My name isn't abel, he said, it's cain, Oh, I like that better than the other one, said lilith, trying to keep the tone of the conversation light, an endeavour that cain laid low with his next words, Abel was the name of my brother, whom I killed because the lord had chosen to favour him at my expense, and I took his name to conceal my own identity, We don't care if you're cain or abel, news of your crime never reached us here, Yes, I see that now, Tell me what happened, Aren't you afraid of me, don't I disgust you, asked cain, You are the man I chose for my bed and with whom, in a little while, I will again lie down. Then cain opened the ark of secrets and described the dramatic event in detail, including the flies on abel's eyes and mouth, as well as the words spoken by the lord, and the enigmatic promise he had made to protect him from a violent death, Don't ask me why he made that promise, said cain, he didn't tell me and I'm not sure there is an explanation, It's enough for me that you're alive and in my arms, said lilith, Don't you see in me a criminal who can never be pardoned, asked cain, No, she said, I see in you a man against whom the lord offended, and now that I know your real name, let's go to bed, I'll burn up with desire right here if you don't hurry, I knew you as abel, and now I need to know you as cain. When the delirium of repeated and various penetrations finally gave way to lassitude, to complete physical exhaustion, lilith said, It was noah, wasn't it, Yes, I believe it must have been, agreed cain, I can't think of any other person in the palace or the city who would want to see me dead as much as he would, When we get up, said lilith, I will send for him, and you will hear what I have to say. They slept a little to rest their weary limbs and woke almost at the same moment. Lilith, already out of bed, said, Stay here, he won't come in. She summoned a

slave-woman to help her dress and then asked the same slave
to send a message to noah, requesting an interview. She sat
in the antechamber waiting, and when her husband arrived,
she said point-blank, You will order the execution of the
slave whom you gave to me as a companion for cain on his
walks, Who's cain, asked noah, taken by surprise, Cain was
abel and now he's cain, you will have the men who ambushed
him killed as well, Where is cain, since that is now his name,
He's safe in my bedroom. The silence became palpable. Then
noah said, I had nothing to do with what you say happened,
Be careful, noah, lying is the worst of all cowardices, But
I'm not lying, You're a coward and you're lying, you're the
one who told the slave what to do and where and how, the
same slave, I suspect, whom you have used to spy on my
activities, hardly necessary since whatever I do, I do openly,
As your husband, you should respect me, Yes, you may be
right, I really should, So what are you waiting for, asked
noah, feigning an irritation which he was far from feeling,
for he was still trembling from her accusation, Oh, I'm not
waiting for anything, I simply don't respect you, Is it because
I'm not a good lover and haven't given you the child you
wanted, he asked, Even if you were a brilliant lover and had
given me not one child but ten, I still wouldn't respect you,
Why, Let me think about it, and as soon as I've discovered
the reasons why I feel not the slightest respect for you, I'll
tell you, you'll be the first to know, I promise, but now,
please leave me, I'm tired and need to rest. Noah was about
to go, when she added, One other thing, when you have
tracked down that wretched traitor, and I hope you will not

be long about it, be sure to tell me so that I can witness his death, the others don't interest me, All right, said noah, and as he crossed the threshold, he heard his wife's last words, And if you torture him, I want to be there too. Back in her room, lilith asked cain, Did you hear, Yes, What did you think, He was clearly the person who ordered me to be killed, he couldn't even act the innocent. Lilith got into bed, but instead of snuggling up to cain, she lay on her back, eyes wide open, staring at the ceiling, then suddenly she said, I have an idea, What, We should kill noah, That's madness, complete nonsense, protested cain, please, don't even think such an absurd thing, Why is it absurd, we would be free of him then, we could get married, you would be the new lord of the city and I would be your queen and your favourite slave, the one who would kiss the ground you walk on, the one who, if necessary, would receive your faeces in her hands, But who would kill him, You would, No, lilith, please don't ask me that, don't order me to do that, I've had my fill of murders, You mean you wouldn't kill him for me, don't you love me, she asked, I who gave you my body so that you could enjoy it endlessly, freely, extravagantly, so that you could enjoy it without rules or prohibitions, I opened to you the doors of my mind, which I had always kept bolted shut, and yet you refuse to do the one thing I ask of you and that would bring us total freedom, Freedom, yes, but remorse too, You're forgetting that I am lilith, I'm not the kind of woman to feel remorse, that's for the weak and feeble, And I am merely a man called cain who came from far away, a man who killed his own brother, who worked as

55

a treader of mud, and who, having done nothing whatever to deserve it, has had the extraordinary good fortune to sleep in the bed of the most beautiful, passionate woman in the world, whom he loves, wants and desires with every pore of his body, So we won't kill noah, then, asked lilith, If you really want to, have a slave do it, No, I don't despise noah so much that I would send a slave to kill him, But I'm a slave and you wanted me to kill him, That's different, a man who lies in my bed is not a slave, or perhaps he is, but only to me and my body, So why don't you kill him yourself, asked cain, Because, despite everything, I don't think I would be capable, Men kill women every day, who knows, perhaps by killing him you would start a new trend, Let other women do that, I am lilith, wild, crazy lilith, but that is as far as my errors and crimes go, So we'll let him live then, it will be punishment enough for him to know that we know he wanted to kill me, Put your arms around me, trample me beneath your feet, o treader of mud. Cain put his arms around her, but he entered her very gently, without violence, with an unexpected tenderness that brought her almost to the verge of tears. Two weeks later, lilith announced that she was pregnant.

Some might say that social and domestic peace finally reigned in the palace, enfolding everyone in the same fraternal embrace. This, however, was not the case, for after a few days had passed, cain came to the conclusion that with lilith expecting a child, his time there had ended. When the child came into the world, everyone would consider it to be noah's child, and although, at first, there would be no shortage of more than justified suspicions and murmurings, time, the great leveller, would soon smooth them away, and future historians would take care to eliminate from the city's chronicle any reference to a certain treader of mud called abel, or cain, or whatever the devil his name was, a doubt which would, in itself, be deemed reason enough to condemn him to oblivion, to permanent quarantine, to the limbo of those events which, for the peace of mind of dynasties, it is best not to talk about. Our story may not be historical, but it shows how wrong or perhaps malicious those historians were, because cain did exist, he gave noah's wife a child, and now he has a problem, how to tell lilith that he wants to leave. He hoped that the lord's curse, You will be a fugitive and a vagabond upon the earth, would persuade her to accept his decision. In the end, though, it proved less problematic than he had thought, perhaps also because the child, that handful of hesitant cells, was already expressing a will and a desire, the first effect of which was to reduce its parents' mad passion for each other to the status of a vulgar sexual fling to which, as we know, the official history will not devote a single line. Cain asked lilith for a donkey and she gave orders for him to be given the very best, the most docile and the sturdiest in the palace stables. At that point, news came that the treacherous slave and his partners in crime had been discovered and arrested. Fortunately for sensitive souls, who always look away from unpleasantnesses of any kind, there were no interrogations and no torture, perhaps because of lilith's pregnancy, for in the opinion of notable local female authorities, this would augur ill for the future of the gestating child, not just the blood that would inevitably be spilled, but also the terrible screams of the torture victims. These authorities, mainly midwives of long experience, believed that a baby in its mother's womb can hear everything going on outside. The result was a sober death by hanging before the entire populace of the city, as a warning, Be careful, this is the very least that could happen to you. The execution was watched from a palace balcony by noah, lilith and cain, the latter because he had been the target of the failed attack. It was noted that, contrary to protocol, noah did not stand in the middle of that small group, lilith did, thus keeping husband and lover apart, as if she were saying that, although she did not love her official spouse, she would remain joined to him, because that is what public opinion seemed to want and what the interests of the dynasty appeared to need, and that although she was being forced by cruel destiny, by the lord's curse, You will be a fugitive and a vagabond upon the earth, to allow cain to leave, she would remain bound to him by the body's sublime memory, by the inextinguishable recollection of the dazzling hours she had spent with him, something a woman never forgets, not like men, to whom such things are like water off a duck's back. The corpses of the malefactors will remain hanging where they are until all that remains of them are bones, for their flesh is accursed, and the earth, if they were buried in it, would erupt and vomit them up, over and over. That night, lilith and cain slept together for the last time. She wept, he clung to her and wept too, but their tears did not last long, they were soon overcome by erotic passion, in whose grip they once more lost all control and fell into delirium, absolute and utter, as if the world were nothing more than that, two lovers interminably devouring each other, so much so that lilith said at last, Kill me. Yes, perhaps that would be the logical end to this story of the love between cain and lilith, but he didn't kill her. He placed a long, lingering kiss on her lips, looked at her for the last time and then went and spent the rest of the night in the bed reserved for him in the antechamber.

6

Despite the grey gloom of pre-dawn, you could see that the birds, not the charming winged creatures that will soon be singing their songs to the sun, but the brutish birds of prey, those carnivores who travel from scaffold to scaffold, had begun their work of public cleansing on the exposed parts of the hanged men, their faces, eyes, hands, feet, the half of a leg left uncovered by a tunic. Two owls, startled by the sound of the ass's hooves, flew up from the dead slave's shoulders with a silken murmur perceptible only to experienced ears. They swooped very low down a narrow alleyway next to the palace and disappeared. Cain dug his heels into the donkey's sides and crossed the square, wondering if he would again meet the old man with the two sheep, and, for the first time, he asked himself who that impertinent person might be, Perhaps it was the lord, he murmured, he'd be quite capable of such a thing, given his liking for turning up when and where he's least expected. He preferred not to think about lilith. When he woke in his lonely guard's bed after a broken, constantly interrupted night's sleep, he had felt a sudden impulse to go into the bedroom for one last word of farewell, one last kiss, and who knows what else. There was still time. Everyone was asleep in the palace, only lilith was sure to be awake, no one would notice his brief incursion, or perhaps only the two slave-women who had half-opened the gates of paradise to him when he first arrived, and they would simply say with a smile, How well we understood you, abel. Once he turns the next corner, the palace will disappear from view. The old man with the sheep wasn't there, the lord, if it was him, was clearly giving cain carte blanche, but no road map or passport or recommendations for hotels and restaurants, it was how journeys used to be made, leaving things to chance or, as they used to say even then, in the lap of the gods. Cain again spurred his donkey on and soon found himself in open countryside. The city had become a dull grey-brown stain, which, gradually, with increasing distance, and even though the donkey was moving at only a moderate pace, seemed to merge with the earth. The landscape was dry, arid, with not so much as a thread of water in sight. Faced by such desolation, it was inevitable that cain would remember the hard journey on foot he had made after the lord drove him out of the fateful valley where poor abel would remain for ever. With nothing to eat and no water to drink, apart from that which miraculously fell from the sky just when his soul had lost all strength and his legs were threatening to give way beneath him. At least this time he would not lack for food, the saddle-bags are crammed full, a loving thought on the part of lilith, who, it would seem, was not such a bad housewife as her dissolute ways might lead one to believe. The problem is that there is not a scrap of shade to be had anywhere. By mid-morning, the sun is already pure fire and the air a shimmering mass that makes us doubt what our eyes can see. Cain said, At least I won't have to go to the trouble of dismounting in order to eat. The road rose and rose, and the donkey, who was clearly no ass, was following a zigzag path, now to the right, now to the left, and one imagines that he must have learned this trick from mules, who know all there is to know about mountain-climbing. A few more steps and they had reached the summit. And to cain's surprise, astonishment and stupefaction, the landscape that lay before him was completely different, full of every imaginable shade of green, with leafy trees and cultivated fields, glittering water, a mild temperature, and white clouds drifting across the sky. He looked back and saw that nothing had changed, the same parched, arid scene lay behind him. It was as if there were a frontier, a line separating the two countries, Or two different times, said cain, unaware that he had said anything, as if someone else were thinking for him. He looked up at the sky and saw that the clouds moving in the direction from which we have come stopped precisely at that point and then, by some unknown art, vanished. We must bear in mind the fact that cain is ill-informed about cartographical matters, one might even say that this, in a way, is his first trip abroad, and so it is only natural that he should feel surprise at seeing other lands, other people, other skies and other customs. That's all very well, but what no one can explain to me is why the clouds cannot pass from here to there. Unless, says the voice issuing from cain's mouth, this is a different time, and this land cared-for and cultivated by the hand of man was once, in ages past, as sterile and desolate as the land of nod. So are we in the future, then, we ask, having seen a few films and read a few books on the subject. Yes, that is the usual formula used to explain what appears to have happened here, the future, we say, and we breathe more easily, now that we have placed a label on it, a docket, but, in our opinion, it would be clearer to call it another present, because the land is the same, but has various presents, some are past presents, others are future presents, and that, surely, is simple enough for anyone to understand. The creature who appears to feel the greatest joy at this change is the donkey. Born and bred in drought-stricken lands, fed on straw and thistles, with water often rationed, or almost, the vision before him verged on the sublime. It's a shame there was no one there capable of inter-preting the twitchings of his ears, that form of semaphore with which nature had endowed him, never thinking that the fortunate beast would one day have to express the in-effable, and the ineffable, as we know, is precisely that which cannot be expressed. Cain is happy too, dreaming of eating his lunch in a countryside full of greenery, babbling brooks and a symphony of little birds warbling away in the branches. Indeed, to the right-hand side of the road, he can see a line of large trees, promising the best of shades and siestas. Cain and the donkey trotted off in that direction. The place would seem to have been created on purpose to provide cool shade for weary travellers and their respective beasts of burden. Running parallel to the trees was a line of bushes that concealed a narrow path going up to the top of the steep

63

hill. Relieved of the weight of the saddlebags, the donkey had surrendered to the delights of lush grass and the occasional rustic flower, neither of which he had ever tasted before. Cain took his time choosing his lunch menu and ate it right there, seated on the ground, surrounded by innocent birds pecking up the crumbs, while memories of blissful moments spent in lilith's arms once more heated his blood. His eyelids were just beginning to droop when he was startled into wakefulness by the voice of a young boy calling, Father, this was followed by a much older male voice asking, What is it, isaac, We have the fire and the wood, but where is the lamb for the burnt offering, and the father replied, The lord will provide a lamb as the burnt offering. And they continued on up the hill. While they are doing so, it would be as well to know how all this began, as further proof that the lord is not a person to be trusted. About three days ago, at most, he had said to abraham, the father of the young boy carrying the firewood on his back, Take your only son, isaac, whom you love, and go into the land of moriah and offer him up for a burnt offering upon one of the mountains, later I will tell you which one. Yes, you read correctly, the lord ordered abraham to sacrifice his own son, and he did so as naturally as if he were asking for a glass of water to slake his thirst, which means it was a deep-seated habit of his. The logical, natural and simply human response would have been for abraham to tell the lord to piss off, but that isn't what happened. The following morning, that unnatural father rose early to saddle up the donkey, prepared wood for the sacrificial fire and set off to the place the lord had indicated, taking with him two servants and his son isaac. On the third day of the journey, abraham saw the aforementioned mountain from afar. He then told his servants, Stay here with the donkey, the lad and I will go over yonder to worship the lord and then come again to you. In short, as well as being as big a son of a bitch as the lord, abraham was a consummate liar, ready to deceive anyone with his forked tongue, which in this case, according to the personal dictionary belonging to the narrator of this story, means treacherous, perfidious, false, disloyal and other similarly fine qualities. When he reached the place of which the lord had spoken, abraham built an altar and placed the wood on it. He then tied up his son and lifted him on to the altar, on top of the wood. Without pausing, he took up his knife in order to sacrifice the poor boy and was just about to slit his throat when he felt a hand grip his arm and heard a voice in his ear shouting, What are you doing, you wretch, killing your own son, burning him, it's the same old story, it starts with a lamb and ends with the murder of the very person you should love most, But the lord told me to do it, said abraham, struggling, Keep still, or I'll be the one who does the killing, untie that boy at once, then kneel down and beg his forgiveness, Who are you, My name is cain, I'm the angel who saved isaac's life. This isn't true, cain is no angel, that title belongs to the being who has just landed with a great flapping of wings and who is now declaiming like an actor who has finally heard his cue, Lay not thy hand upon the lad, nor do anything to him, for now I know that thou fearest the lord, being prepared, for love of him, to sacrifice even your only son, You're late, said cain, the only reason isaac isn't dead is because I stepped in to prevent it. The angel looked suitably contrite, I'm terribly sorry to be late, but it really wasn't my fault, I was on my way here when I developed a mechanical problem in my right wing, it was out of synch with the left one, and the result was that I got completely turned around, in fact I wasn't even sure I would get here, and given that no one had told me which of these mountains had been chosen as the place of sacrifice, it's a miracle I arrived at all, You're late, said cain again, Better late than never, replied the angel smugly, as if he had uttered a great truth, That's where you're wrong, never is not the opposite of late, the opposite of late is too late, retorted cain. The angel muttered, Oh, no, a rationalist, and since he had not yet completed the mission with which he had been charged, he rattled off the rest of his message, This is what the lord commanded me to say: since you were capable of doing this and did not withhold your own son, I swear by my good name that I will bless you and multiply your seed as the stars of the heavens and as the sand upon the seashore and they will possess the gates of his enemies, and in your seed shall all the nations of the earth be blessed because you have obeyed my voice, the word of the lord, That, for those who don't know it or pretend to ignore it, is the lord's double accounting system, said cain, whereby one man can win and the other not lose, apart from that, I don't see why all the people of the earth will be blessed just because abraham obeyed a stupid order, That is what we in heaven call due obedience, said the angel. Dragging his right wing, and with a bad taste in his mouth after the failure of his mission, the celestial creature departed, and abraham and his son are also walking back to where their servants are waiting for them, and now, while cain is once again loading the saddle-bags on to his donkey, let us imagine a dialogue between the would-be executioner and his victim saved at the last moment. Isaac asked, Father, whatever did I do to you that would make you want to kill me, your only son, You did nothing wrong, isaac, So why did you want to cut my throat as if I were a lamb, asked the boy, if that man, may the lord's blessings be upon him, hadn't come and grabbed your arm, you would now be carrying home a corpse, It was the lord's idea, he meant it as a test, A test of what, Of my faith and my obedience, What kind of lord would order a father to kill his own son, He's the only lord we have, the lord of our ancestors, the lord who was here when we were born, And if that lord had a son, would he order him to be killed as well, asked isaac, Time will tell, So the lord is capable of anything, of good, bad and worse, Yes, he is, What would have happened if you had disobeyed the order, asked isaac, Well, the lord usually sends down ruin or disease upon anyone who fails him, So the lord is vengeful, Yes, I think he is, said abraham quietly, as if he were afraid of being heard, nothing is impossible for the lord, Not even error and crime, asked isaac, Especially error and crime, Father, I don't understand this religion, But you have to, my son, you have no option, and now I must make a request, a humble request, What is it, Let us forget what happened here, Well, I'm not sure I can, father, I can still see myself lying, bound, on top of the pyre, and your arm raised, the blade of the knife glinting, That wasn't me, I would never do such a thing when in my right mind, Do you mean that the lord makes people mad, asked isaac, Yes, he often does, almost always, replied abraham, Even if that were true, you were still the one with the knife in your hand, The lord had everything organised, he would have intervened at the last moment, after all, you saw the angel, The angel arrived late, Yes, but the lord would have found some other way of saving you, he probably even knew that the angel was going to be late and that's why he had that man appear, Cain his name was, don't forget the debt you owe him, Cain, repeated abraham obediently, I knew him before you were born, The man who saved your own son from having his throat slit and being burned on the very firewood he had carried on his back, But neither of those things happened, my son, Father, it isn't so much a matter of whether or not I died, although obviously that matters to me a great deal, but the fact that we are ruled by such a lord, as cruel as baal, who devours his own children, Where did you hear the name baal, In dreams, father. I'm dreaming, said cain when he opened his eyes. He had fallen asleep while he rode and had suddenly woken up. He was in the middle of a very different landscape, with earth as parched as in the land of nod, although the ground was sandy rather than covered in thistles, and with only a few scrawny trees for vegetation. Another present, he said. It seemed to him that this must be an older present than the previous one, the one in which he had saved the life of the boy called isaac, and this indicated that he could go forwards as well as backwards in time, although not at his own bidding, for, to be frank, he felt like someone who, more or less, but only more or less, knows where he is, but not where he is heading. Just to give an example of the difficulties cain faces in orienting himself, this place looks to be a present that happened a long time ago, as if the world were in the last phase of being built and everything still had a rather temporary feel about it. For example, in the distance, on the far horizon, he can make out a very tall tower, like a truncated cone, that is, a conical form, the top of which had been sliced off or not yet put in place. It was a long way away, but it seemed to cain, who had excellent eyesight, that there were people moving around the building. Curiosity made him spur the donkey on, but then prudence caused him to rein him in again. He couldn't be sure that those were peace-loving people, and even if they were, who knows what might happen to a donkey laden with two saddlebags of the finest quality food when confronted by a multitude of people who, by necessity or tradition, were ready to devour anything and everything set before them. He didn't know them, had no idea who they were, but it wasn't hard to imagine. Anyway, he clearly couldn't leave the donkey there, tied to one of those trees like some worthless object, for he risked finding neither donkey nor food when he returned. Caution told him to take another route and to cease his adventuring and warned him, in short, not to defy blind fate. Curiosity, however, proved stronger than caution. He stuffed the tops of the saddlebags with twigs to make it look as if the bags contained only animal feed, and then, alea jacta est, set off towards the tower. As he approached, the sound of voices, faint at first, began growing and growing until it became a hubbub. They seem like madmen, like complete maniacs, thought cain. Yes, they were mad, but with desperation because they spoke but could not understand each other, as if they were deaf and had to keep speaking louder and louder, but in vain. They were all speaking different languages and some of them even laughed and made fun of the others as if their own language was more musical and more beautiful than anyone else's. The odd thing is, as cain did not yet know, none of those languages had existed in the world before, all the people there had once spoken only one language and had understood each other without the slightest difficulty. Cain was fortunate enough to meet a man who spoke hebrew, the language that had fallen to him to speak in the midst of all that deliberately created confusion, the scale of which cain was just beginning to grasp, with people talking, without the aid of dictionaries or interpreters, in english, german, french, spanish, italian, basque, some in latin and greek and even, who would have thought it, in portuguese. Why all this discord, asked cain, and the man replied, When we came from the east to settle here, we all spoke the same language, And what was that language called, asked cain, Since it was the only one, it didn't need a name, it was just language, So what happened, Someone had the idea of making bricks and firing them in a kiln, And how did you make them, asked the former treader of mud, feeling that he was among his own people, Just as we had always done, with clay, sand

70

and grit, and for mortar we used mud, And then, Then we decided to build a city with a large tower, that one over there, a tower that would reach up to the sky, What for, asked cain, So that we would be famous, And what happened, why did you stop building, Because the lord came to see it and was displeased, Reaching heaven is what all good men desire, surely the lord should have given you a helping hand, If only he had, but that isn't what happened, So what did he do, He said that once we had built the tower, we would be capable of doing whatever we wanted, which is why he mixed up all the languages and why, from then on, as you see, we could no longer understand each other, And now, asked cain, Now there will be no city, the tower will never be finished and we, each with our own language, will be unable to live together as we once did, It would be best to leave the tower as a reminder, there will come a time when people will travel from all over to visit the ruins, There probably won't be any ruins left, because there are those who say that once we've left, the lord will send a great wind to destroy it, and what the lord says, he does, His great fault is jealousy, instead of being proud of his children, he succumbed to envy, and he obviously can't bear to see anyone happy, All that toil and sweat for nothing, What a shame, said cain, it would have been a fine tower, Yes, said the man, fixing greedy eyes on cain's donkey. And it would have been easy enough for him to make off with it had he asked for the help of his companions, but selfishness won out over intelligence. When he made a move to grab the halter, the donkey, who had always had a reputation for docility in noah's

71

stables, performed a kind of dance step with his front feet, then turned his back on the man and unleashed a kick that sent the poor devil flying. Although he had acted in legitimate self-defence, the donkey was immediately aware that this eminently good reason would be unacceptable to the advancing mob who, crying out in all the languages under the sun, were poised to steal the saddlebags and make mincemeat of him. He didn't need his rider to dig in his heels, but set off at a lively trot which, given his asinine nature, became an even more unexpected gallop, for donkeys may be reliable beasts, but they are not noted for their speed. The assailants had to resign themselves to seeing him disappear in a cloud of dust, which would have another important consequence, that of transporting cain and his mount into another future present in that same place, free of any of the lord's bold rivals, who were about to be scattered throughout the world because they no longer had a common language to bind them together. Imposing, majestic, the tower was still visible on the far horizon, and although unfinished, it nonetheless looked set to defy the centuries and the millennia, then, suddenly, one moment it was there and the next it wasn't. The lord was carrying out his threat, which was to send a great wind that would not leave stone on stone or brick on brick. Cain was too far away to feel the violence of the hurricane blown from the mouth of the lord or the roar of the walls toppling one after the other, the pillars, the arcades, the vaults, the buttresses, and so the tower appeared to collapse in silence, like a house of cards, until all that remained was a vast cloud of dust that rose up to the sky and obscured the sun. Many years later, people would say that a meteorite had fallen there, a celestial body, of the many that wander about in space, but that isn't true, it was the tower of babel, which the lord, out of pride, would not allow to be completed. The history of mankind is the history of our misunderstandings with god, for he doesn't understand us, and we don't understand him.

7

It was written on the tablets of fate that cain would meet abraham again. One day, on yet another of those sudden time-travelling shifts from present to present, now forwards, now backwards, cain found himself at the hottest hour of the day outside a tent near the oaks of mamre. He thought he had caught sight of an old man who vaguely reminded him of someone he knew. In order to be sure, he called at the door of the tent and abraham appeared. Are you looking for someone, he asked, Well, yes and no, I was just passing through, when it seemed to me that I recognised you, and I was right, I'm cain, how is your son isaac, You're mistaken, the only son I have is called ishmael, not isaac, and ishmael is the child I had by my slave hagar. Cain's sharp wits, accustomed to such situations, immediately came into play, this game of alternative presents had once again manipulated time and shown him what would happen at a later date before it actually did, which, put in simpler, more explicit terms means that isaac had not yet been born. I don't recall ever having seen you before, said abraham, but come in, make yourself at home, I'll get a servant to bring you water to wash your feet and give you some bread for the journey,

First, I must tend to the needs of my donkey, Take him over to those oak trees, where you'll find hay and straw and a drinking trough full of fresh water. Cain did as abraham suggested and, tethering the donkey in the shade, he removed the saddle to give the animal some relief from the heat. Then he felt the almost empty saddlebags and wondered what he could do to remedy what was fast becoming an alarming lack of food. Abraham's words had given him new hope, but man cannot live by bread alone, especially one who has grown used to gastronomic delicacies far above his original station and social class. Leaving the donkey to enjoy the most basic of country pleasures, water, shade and plentiful food, cain returned to the tent, called out to announce his presence and then went in. He saw at once that some kind of meeting was going on, to which, of course, he had not been invited. Abraham was in conversation with three men, who had apparently arrived in the meantime. Cain made as if to withdraw discreetly, but abraham said, Don't leave, sit down, you are all my guests, and now, if you'll permit me, I must go and give my orders. He went into a room in the back of the tent and said to sarah, his wife, Quick, knead three measures of the best flour and make a few loaves. Then he went to the area where the cattle were kept and brought in a plump young calf, which he handed over to a servant to be slaughtered and cooked. When all this had been done, he served his guests the veal that had been prepared, saying to cain, Join us under the trees. And as if that were not generosity enough, he served them butter and milk as well. Then the men asked, Where is sarah, and abraham replied,

She is in the tent. That was when one of the three men said, I will return to your house within a year and, at the appointed time, your wife will give birth to a son. That will be isaac, said cain in a low voice, so low that no one seemed to hear. Now abraham and sarah were well on in years, and she was no longer of child-bearing age. That is why she laughed and thought, How could I possibly have that pleasure again now that my husband and I are old and weary. The man asked abraham, Why did sarah laugh, believing that she cannot have a son at her age, when nothing is too hard for the lord. And he repeated what he had said before, I will return to your house within a year and, at the appointed time, your wife will give birth to a son. When she heard this, sarah was afraid and denied that she had laughed, but the man said, Nay, but you did laugh. At that moment, everyone realised that the third man present was the lord god in person. We forgot to mention that, before going into the tent, cain had pulled the edge of his turban low over his forehead to hide the mark from curious eyes, especially from the lord, whom he immediately recognised, and so when the lord asked if his name was cain, he answered, Yes, it is, but I'm not that cain.

Faced by this none too clever evasion, one would have expected the lord to have insisted and for cain to end up confessing that he was indeed the same cain who had murdered his brother abel and therefore been condemned for ever to be a wanderer and a fugitive, but the lord had more urgent and important things to deal with than finding out the true identity of a somewhat suspicious stranger.

For in heaven, whence he had come only moments before, he had heard numerous complaints about the crimes against nature committed in the nearby cities of sodom and gomorrah. As the impartial judge he had always prided himself on being, although it must be said that there have been no shortage of actions on his part to show exactly the opposite, he had come down to earth in order to find out the truth of the matter. This is why he was now travelling to sodom, accompanied by abraham and by cain, who had asked, as a curious tourist, if he could come along too. The men with the lord, who were clearly his angel companions, had gone on ahead. Then abraham asked the lord three questions, Will you destroy the innocent along with the guilty, what if there are fifty innocent people in the city, will you also destroy them and not spare the whole city for the sake of those fifty innocent souls. And he went on, saying, You cannot do such a thing, lord, you cannot slay the innocent along with the guilty, if you do, it will seem, in everyone's eyes, that being innocent and guilty are one and the same, and you, who are the judge of all the earth, must be just in your sentences. To which the lord responded, If I find in the city of sodom fifty innocent people, I will spare the whole city for their sake. Encouraged and full of hope, abraham went on, Since I have taken the liberty of speaking so freely to the lord, I who am nothing but dust and ashes, allow me one more question, what if there are not quite fifty innocent people, but only forty-five, will you destroy the whole city for the lack of five. The lord answered, If I find forty-five innocent people there, I will not destroy the city. Abraham decided to strike again while the iron was hot, What if there are only forty innocent people, to which the lord answered, For the sake of those forty people, I will not destroy the city, And what if there are only thirty, For the sake of those thirty, I will not destroy the city, And what if there are only twenty, For the sake of those twenty, I will not destroy the city. Then abraham went further, Please don't be angry with me if I ask one further thing, Speak, said the lord, What if there are only ten innocent people, and the lord answered, For the sake of those ten, I will not destroy the city. Having thus responded to abraham's questions, the lord withdrew, and abraham, accompanied by cain, returned to the tent. Nothing more was said of isaac, the son yet to be born. When they reached the oaks of mamre, abraham went into his tent and re-emerged shortly afterwards with the promised loaves. Cain stopped saddling up his donkey in order to thank abraham for this generous gift, and asked, How do you think the lord is going to count the ten innocent people, who, assuming they exist, will prevent the destruction of sodom, do you think he will go from door to door, asking fathers and their male descendants about their sexual proclivities and appetites, The lord doesn't need to do that, he only has to look down on the city from above to know what is going on, answered abraham, Do you mean that the lord made that agreement with you for no reason other than to please you, cain asked again, The lord gave his word, Well, as sure as my name is cain, although admittedly I have also been known as abel, I'm not convinced, I reckon that, regardless of whether there are innocent people living there or not, sodom will still be destroyed, possibly tonight, Yes, that's possible, and not only sodom either, but gomorrah and two or three other cities of the plain, where sexual customs have become equally lax, with men going with men and women being left to one side, Aren't you worried about what might happen to those two men who came with the lord, They weren't men, they were angels, for I know them well, Angels without wings, They won't need wings if they need to escape, Well, if the men of sodom lay hands or indeed anything else on them, I don't think they'll care a jot whether they're angels or not, and the lord will be most displeased, if I were you, I would go to the city to see what's happened, they won't harm you, Yes, you're right, I'll go, but I would feel safer if you came with me, one and a half men are better than one, But we're two, not one and a half, Oh, I'm only half a man now, cain, In that case, let's go, and if they attack us, I could probably despatch two or three of them with the knife I have under my tunic, otherwise, we'll just have to hope that the lord will provide. Then abraham summoned a servant and ordered him to take cain's donkey to the stables. And he said to cain, If you have no plans that require you to leave today, I will offer you my hospitality for the night as a small recompense for being kind enough to accompany me, If it is in my power, I hope to be able to do you more favours in the future, said cain, but abraham could not grasp the meaning that lay behind those mysterious words. They set off to the city, and abraham said, Let us go first to the house of my nephew lot, son of my brother haran, he will tell us what has been going on. The sun had already set when they reached sodom, but it was still light. They saw a huge rowdy crowd gathered outside lot's house, We want to see the men you took into your house, bring them out to us, that we may know them, and they pounded on the door, threatening to break it down. Abraham said, Come with me, there's another entrance at the back. They entered just as lot, barricaded in behind his front door, was saying, Please, my friends, do not commit such a crime, I have two unmarried daughters, you can do what you like with them, but do not harm these men who sought shelter in my house. The crowd outside continued shouting furiously, but suddenly their cries became lamentations and tears, I'm blind, I'm blind, they were all saying and asking, Where is the door, there was a door here and now it's gone. To save his angels from being brutally raped, a fate worse than death according to those who know, the lord blinded all the men of sodom without exception, which proves that there could not have been even ten innocent men in the whole city. In the house, the visitors were saying to lot, Leave this place along with all the members of your family, your sons, daughters, sons-in-law, and everything else you have in the city, because we have come here to destroy it. Lot went out and warned his future sons-in-law, but they did not believe him and laughed at what they judged to be a joke. It was dawn when the messengers of the lord said again to lot, Take your wife and your two remaining daughters and leave the city if you do not wish to be punished as well, for while that is not the lord's will, it is exactly what will happen if you do not obey. Then, without waiting for an answer, they took him, his wife and his daughters by the hand and led them out of the city. Abraham and cain went with them, although not into the mountains which is where lot and his family would have gone had they followed the angel's advice, for lot asked instead to be allowed to stay in a small town, almost a village, called zoar. Go, said the messengers, but do not look back. Lot entered the town when the sun was coming up. Then the lord rained down fire and brimstone upon sodom and upon gomorrah and razed both to the ground, destroying all the inhabitants and everything that grew there. Wherever you looked, you could see only ruins, ashes and charred bodies. As for lot's wife, she disobeyed the order not to look back and was transformed into a pillar of salt. No one has ever been able to understand why she was punished in that way, for it is only natural to want to know what is going on behind you. It's possible that the lord wanted to punish curiosity as if it were a mortal sin, but that doesn't say much for his intelligence either, just look at what happened with the tree of the knowledge of good and evil, if eve hadn't given adam some of the fruit to eat, if she hadn't eaten it herself, they would still be in the garden of eden, and we know how boring that was. On the way back, they happened to stop for a moment on the road where abraham had spoken to the lord, and cain said, There's an idea I can't get out of my head, What's that, asked abraham, There must have been innocent people in sodom and in the other cities that were burned, If so, the lord would have kept the promise he made to me to save their lives, What about the children, said cain, surely the children were innocent, Oh my god, murmured abraham and his voice was like a groan, Yes, your god perhaps, but not theirs.

8

In an instant, the same cain who had just left sodom, travelling along proper roads, was suddenly transported to the sinai desert where, to his great surprise, he found himself in the midst of a multitude of thousands all encamped at the foot of a mountain. He had no idea who they were, nor where they had come from, nor where they were going. If he were to ask any of the people next to him, he would immediately betray the fact that he was a stranger, and that might bring him all kinds of embarrassments and problems. Keeping prudently on the back foot, therefore, he decided to call himself neither cain nor abel this time, just in case the devil should decide to stir things up and introduce someone who had heard tell of that tale of two brothers and who might then start asking awkward questions. It would be best to keep eyes and ears open and to draw his own conclusions. One thing was certain, the name of moses was on everyone's lips, some uttered it in a tone of ancient veneration, but most did so with a rather more contemporary note of impatience. They were the ones who kept asking, Where is moses, he went up to the mountain to speak to the lord forty days and forty nights ago, and we have received neither word nor command from him since, the lord has obviously abandoned his people and wants nothing more to do with us. The road to self-deception is narrow to begin with, but there's always someone ready to broaden it out, for as the proverb says, self-deception is like eating or scratching, it's all a matter of beginning. Along with those waiting for moses' return from mount sinai was a brother of his called aaron, who had been appointed high priest during the time of the israelites' captivity in egypt. The more impatient among them addressed themselves to him, saying, Since we do not know what has happened to moses, why don't you make us some gods to guide us, and aaron, who was, it would seem, neither a model of steadfastness nor very brave, instead of refusing point-blank, said, If that's what you want, take the gold earrings from your wives and sons and daughters and bring them here. They did as he asked, and he then melted the gold, poured it into a mould, cast it and made of it a golden calf. Apparently pleased with his work and oblivious to the serious confusion he was about to create around that future object of worship, namely, was it the lord himself or a calf replacing him, he announced, Tomorrow we will hold a feast in honour of the lord. Cain heard all this and, piecing together odd words, scraps of dialogue, snatches of opinion, he began to form an idea, not just about what was happening at that moment, but about what had gone on before. He was greatly helped in this by conversations overheard in a tent used as a dormitory for soldiers, those without families of their own. Unable to think of anything better, Cain had told them that his name was noah, and he was made welcome and invited to join in their conversations, for jews have always been a talkative people. The following morning, a rumour spread that moses was finally coming down from mount sinai and that joshua, his aide and the israelites' military commander, had gone to meet him. When joshua heard the shouts of the people, he said to moses, There is a noise of war in the camp, What you hear, said moses, are not the happy songs of victory or the sad songs of defeat, it is merely the sound of people singing. Little did he know what awaited him. When he entered the camp, the first thing he saw was the golden calf and the people dancing round it. He seized the calf, smashed it into pieces and ground it to powder, then, turning to aaron, he asked, What did this people do to you that you allowed them to commit so great a sin, and aaron, who, for all his faults, knew the world in which he lived, replied, Do not be angry with me, for you know that these people are set on mischief, it was their idea, they wanted other gods because they no longer believed that you would return, and they would probably have killed me if I had refused to do as they asked. Then moses stood at the gate of the camp and cried, Whoever is on the lord's side let him come to me. All the tribe of levi gathered around him, and moses proclaimed, Thus says the lord god of israel, take up your swords, return to the camp and go from door to door killing your brother, your friend, your neighbour. And in this way nearly three thousand men died. And the blood ran between the tents like a flood that had sprung up from the earth, as if the earth itself were bleeding, everywhere lay bodies cleaved in two, with throats slit or guts hanging out, and so loud were the screams of the women and children that they must have reached the top of mount sinai where the lord would be rejoicing in his revenge. Cain could barely believe what he was seeing. Burning sodom and gomorrah to the ground had evidently not been enough for the lord, for here, at the foot of mount sinai, was clear, irrefutable proof of his wickedness, three thousand men killed simply because he was angered by the creation of a supposed rival in the form of a golden calf. I killed one brother and the lord punished me, who, I would like to know, is going to punish the lord for all these deaths, thought cain, lucifer was quite right when he rebelled against god, and those who say he did so out of envy are wrong, he simply recognised god's evil nature. Some of the gold dust blown by the wind stained cain's hands. He washed them in a puddle as if ritually shaking from his feet the dust of a place where he had been ill received, then he climbed on to his donkey and left. A dark cloud hung over mount sinai, where the lord sat.

For reasons it is not in our power to explain, mere repeaters as we are of ancient stories, constantly wavering between the most ingenuous credulity and the most resolute scepticism, cain found himself plunged into what we can, without exaggeration, call a tempest, a calendric cyclone, a temporal hurricane. During the few days following the episode of the golden calf and its brief existence, his ever-changing presents followed one upon another with incredible rapidity, emerging from the void and hurling themselves

86

back into the void in the form of random, disparate images, with no continuity or connection between them, at times showing what appeared to be the battles of a never-ending war whose first cause no one could remember, at others revealing a kind of grotesque and invariably violent farce, a sort of on-going grand guignol, harsh, discordant and obsessive. One of these images, the most enigmatic and fleeting of all, set before his eyes a vast expanse of water where one could see nothing as far as the horizon, not even an island or a sailing boat with its fishermen and their nets. Water, water everywhere, nothing but water covering the earth. Obviously, cain could not have been an eye-witness to all of these stories, and some, whether true or not, came to him via the well-known route of hearing a story from someone who had heard it from someone else who had, in turn, told someone else. One example was the scandalous case of lot and his daughters. When sodom and gomorrah were destroyed, lot was afraid to go on living in the nearby town of zoar and decided to seek shelter in a cave in the mountains. One day, his eldest daughter said to his younger daughter, Our father is old, one day he will die, and there is no man on the earth to marry us, come, let us make our father drink wine and we will lie with him so that he may give us descendants. And so it was, and lot did not notice when she lay down nor when she left his bed, and the same thing happened with his younger daughter on the following night, for he was so old and drunk that, again, he did not notice when she lay down nor when she left his bed. The two sisters duly became pregnant, but when this story was

87

told to cain, that great expert on erections and ejaculations, as lilith, his first and so far only lover, would happily confirm, he said, Any man who was so drunk that he didn't even know what was going on wouldn't even be able to get it up, and if he couldn't get it up, then no penetration could take place and no engendering either. We should not be surprised by the fact that in the ancient societies he had created, the lord should accept incest as an everyday occurrence not deserving of punishment, for nature then lacked any moral code and was concerned only with the propagation of the species, whether driven by natural urges, mere lust or, as people will say later on, simply doing what comes naturally. The lord himself had said, Go forth and multiply, and he put no limits or restrictions on that injunction, nor on who one should or shouldn't go with. It's possible, although this is only a working hypothesis, that the lord's liberality in the matter of making babies had to do with the need to replace the considerable losses suffered, in the way of dead and wounded, by his and other people's armies, as we have already seen and will doubtless continue to see. We need only recall what happened within sight of mount sinai and the column of smoke that was the lord, the erotic zeal with which, that same night, once the survivors had dried their tears, they hurriedly did their best to engender new combatants who would one day wield the ownerless swords and slit the throats of the children of those who had just vanquished them. Look at what happened to the midianites. In the great lottery of war, it chanced that they defeated the israelites, who, in the past, it must be said, despite all

88

the propaganda to the contrary, often faced defeat. This rankled with the lord, like a stone in his shoe, and he said to moses, You should take vengeance for the israelites on the midianites and then, prepare yourself, for afterwards you will be gathered unto your people. Swallowing the unpleasant news about his own imminent demise, moses ordered each of the twelve tribes of israel to provide one thousand men for the war and thus raised an army of twelve thousand soldiers, who destroyed the midianites, not one of whom escaped with his life. Among the dead were the kings of midian, namely evi, rekem, zur, hur and reba, for kings then used to have strange names, rather than being called joão or afonso or manuel, sancho or pedro. As for the women and children, the israelites took them captive, as well as seizing their cattle, sheep, and all their other goods and chattels. They presented this booty to moses and to the priest eleazar and to the congregation of the children of israel, who were encamped on the plains of moab, by the river jordan, near jericho, toponymic details which we give here merely to show that we have invented nothing. On learning the outcome of the battle, moses was angry and he demanded of the soldiers entering the encampment, Why did you not also kill the women who caused the israelites to trespass against the lord and worship instead the god baal, thus causing a plague among the people of the lord, I order you, therefore, to go back and kill every male child and every woman who has lain with a man, and as for the female children and those women who have not yet lain with a man, you may keep them for yourselves. None of this surprised cain. What was new to him was the sharing out of the spoils, which we set down here as an indispensable record of the customs of the day, with apologies to the reader for an excess of detail for which we are not responsible. This is what the lord said to moses, You and the priest eleazar and the chief fathers of the congregation take the sum of the spoils that were taken, both of men and of beasts, and divide them into two parts, half for the soldiers who fought in the battle and the other half for the congregation. From the soldiers' half you will take as a tribute to the lord one soul of every five hundred, both of people and of beasts, oxen, asses or sheep. Of the children of israel's half you will take one portion of every fifty, both of people and of beasts, oxen, asses or sheep, and give them to the levites, who guard the tabernacle of the lord. Moses did as the lord commanded. And the booty that the israelite soldiers took was six hundred and seventy-five thousand sheep, seventy-two thousand oxen, sixty-one thousand asses and thirty-two thousand women who had not lain with men. And the half corresponding to the soldiers who had gone into battle was, therefore, three hundred and thirty-seven thousand five hundred sheep, of which the lord's tribute was six hundred and seventy-five, thirty-six thousand oxen, of which the lord's tribute was seventy-two, thirty thousand five hundred asses, of which the lord's tribute was sixty-one, and sixteen thousand people, of which the lord's tribute was thirty-two. The other half, which moses gave to the israelites, consisted also of three hundred and thirty-seven thousand five hundred sheep, thirty-six thousand oxen, thirty thousand five hundred asses and sixteen thousand women who had not lain with men. Of that half, moses took one portion of every fifty, both of people and of beasts, and just as the lord commanded, he gave them to the levites, who guard the tabernacle of the lord. But this was not all. In gratitude to the lord for having saved their lives, for none of them had died in the battle, the soldiers, through the intermediary of their commanding officers, offered up to the lord the gold they had found during the sack of the town. Those bracelets, bangles, rings, earrings and necklaces weighed in at some three hundred and seventy pounds. As has been amply demonstrated, as well as being naturally gifted with the brain of a book-keeper and being very quick at mental arithmetic too, the lord is also what one can only describe as very rich. Still astonished by the abundance of cattle, slave-women and gold, the fruits of the battle against the midianites, cain thought, War is obviously very good business indeed, perhaps the best of all, to judge by the ease with which, in an instant, one can acquire thousands and thousands of oxen, sheep, asses and women, this lord will one day be known as the god of war, I can see no other use for him, thought cain, and he was right. It is quite possible that the pact that some say exists between god and men contains only two articles, namely, you scratch my back and I'll scratch yours. One thing is sure, things have changed a lot. Once, the lord would appear to us in person, in the flesh so to speak, and even took a certain satisfaction in showing himself to the world, just ask adam and eve, who benefitted from his presence, or ask cain, although that was in less fortunate circumstances, we refer, of course, to the murder of abel, when there was little cause for contentment. Now, though, the lord conceals himself in columns of smoke, as if he preferred not to be seen. As mere observers of events, we are of the view that he feels ashamed of some of his less palatable actions, for example, those innocent children in sodom devoured by his divine fire.

9

The place is the same, but the present has changed. Cain sees before him the city of jericho, which, for reasons of military security, he has not been allowed to enter. The attack by joshua's army is expected at any moment, and, however vehemently cain assured them that he was not an israelite, they continued to deny him access, especially since he could give no satisfactory answer to the question, What are you then, if you're not an israelite. When cain was born, there was no such thing as the israelites, and when, much later, they came into existence, with the sometimes disastrous consequences with which we are familiar, the censuses carried out omitted the family of adam. Cain was not an israelite, but neither was he a hittite, an amorite, a perizzite, a hivite or a jebusite. He was saved from this lack of definition by a farrier from joshua's army, who fell in love with cain's donkey, That's a fine animal you've got there, He's been with me since I left the land of nod and he's never let me down yet, Well, in that case, if you agree, I'll take you on as my assistant on a bed and board basis, on condition that you let me ride your donkey now and then. Cain thought this a reasonable proposal, but asked, And afterwards, After what, asked the other man, After jericho falls, Oh, jericho is just the beginning, afterwards there'll be a long war of conquest during which farriers will be as necessary as soldiers, In that case, I accept, said cain. He had heard tell, from those who had known her, of a famous prostitute who lived in jericho, a certain rahab, whom he longed to meet so as to refresh his blood, for he hadn't had a woman under him since the last night he spent with lilith. And despite not being allowed into jericho, he still did not give up all hope of sleeping with her. The farrier informed the necessary people that he had taken on an unpaid assistant, and thus cain became a member of the support services of joshua's army, entrusted, under the watchful eye of his boss, with the task of treating the saddle sores of donkeys and asses, donkeys and asses and nothing else, you understand, for a cavalry worthy of the name had not yet been invented. After what seemed to everyone an excessively long wait, they were told that the lord had finally spoken to joshua, to whom he had said the following, word for word, For six days, you and your soldiers will march round the city once a day, and seven priests will go ahead of the ark of the covenant, bearing seven ram's horn trumpets, and on the seventh day, you will march round the city seven times and the priests will sound their trumpets, and when they sound a much longer blast, the people must shout with a great shout and then the walls of the city will fall down. Contrary to what a perfectly legitimate scepticism might expect, that is exactly what happened. On the seventh day of that never-before-tried tactic, the walls really did fall down and the soldiers poured into the city through whatever opening lay before them, and jericho was taken. They destroyed everything, putting to the sword men and women, young and old, even oxen and sheep and asses. When cain finally entered the city, the prostitute rahab had vanished with all her family, for they had been taken to a place of safety as a reward for the help she gave to the lord when she hid the two spies joshua had sent into jericho. When he heard this, cain lost all interest in her. Despite his own reprehensible past, he hated traitors, who were, in his opinion, the lowest of the low. Joshua's soldiers set fire to the city and burned everything in it, apart from the silver and gold and the vessels of brass and of iron, which, as usual, were added to the treasury of the house of the lord. That was when joshua issued a second threat, Cursed be the man who rebuilds the city of jericho, death to the eldest son of he who lays the foundations and to the youngest son of the man who sets up the gates. At the time, curses were real literary works of art, both in the force of their intention and in the language in which they were couched, had joshua not been the ruthless person he was, we might almost take him as a stylistic model, at least as regards the important rhetorical chapter on curses and maledictions, so little read in modern times. From there, the israelite army marched on the all too appropriately named city of ai, where, after suffering the humiliation of a defeat, the israelites learned that you don't mess around with the lord god. For a man called achan had taken certain things from jericho that had been condemned to be destroyed and, as a consequence, the anger of the lord was kindled against the israelites, This will not do, he cried, whoever disobeys my orders is condemned. Meanwhile, joshua, led astray by erroneous information given to him by the spies he had sent to ai, made the mistake of underestimating the strength of his adversary and sent fewer than three thousand men into battle, and they, attacked and pursued by the inhabitants of the city, were forced to flee. The israelites lost the will to fight, as has always happened at the slightest defeat, and although they no longer show their dismay in quite the same way as in the days of joshua, rending their clothes and falling to the ground and covering their heads in dust, some verbal wailing is inevitable. It is evident from joshua's pleas and complaints and questions that the lord did a very bad job of bringing these people up. Why did you have us cross the jordan, was it in order to deliver us into the hands of the amorites, to destroy us, it would have been far better if we had stayed on the other side. It was clearly absurd for this same joshua to lose his head over the loss of a mere thirty-six soldiers, the number killed in the attempted attack on ai, when, after every battle, he leaves behind him a trail of many thousands of enemy corpses. And he went on, O lord, if israel flees its enemies, the canaanites and all the inhabitants of the land shall hear of it and will attack us and destroy us, and no one will remember us, what will you do to defend our great name, he asked. The lord did not appear in person or in the form of a column of smoke this time, and so one imagines that he was merely a voice thundering out into space and echoing around the mountains and the valleys, saying, The israelites have sinned, you have broken the covenant

I made with you, you have taken things that were destined to be destroyed, you have stolen them and hidden them and put them among your baggage. The voice grew louder, That is why you could not resist your enemies, because you, too, were condemned to be destroyed, and I will not take your side again until you destroy that which, though condemned to destruction, is still in your possession, up, joshua, and summon the people, the man who is found to have taken those things will be burned along with everything he has, family and goods. Early the next morning, joshua gave orders for the people to come before him, household by household. Questions, enquiries and denunciations finally led him to a man called achan, the son of carmi, the son of zabdi, the son of serah, of the tribe of judah. Joshua addressed him in gentle, mellifluous tones, saying, My son, give glory to the lord and make confession to him, tell me what you have done, hide nothing from me. Cain, who was watching along with the others, thought, They're sure to pardon him, joshua wouldn't speak to him like that if he was going to condemn him. Meanwhile, achan was saying, It's true, I have sinned against the lord god of israel, Speak, tell me everything, joshua urged him, When I saw among the spoils a beautiful babylonian cloak, and nearly two hundred shekels of silver and a wedge of gold nearly fifty shekels in weight, then I coveted them and took them, Tell me, where are those things now, asked joshua, They are buried in the earth beneath my tent, and the silver under them. Having wheedled this confession out of him, joshua sent some men to search the tent where they found the stolen items, with the silver underneath, just as achan had said. They took them and brought them to joshua and to all the israelites and placed them before the lord, or, rather, before the ark of the covenant that stood for him. Joshua then took achan with the silver, the cloak and the wedge of gold, along with his sons and daughters, and his oxen and his asses and his sheep, his tent and all that he had, and led them to the valley of achor. When they arrived, joshua said, You were the cause of our misfortune, because of you, thirty-six israelites died, may the lord now be the cause of your misfortune. Then the other israelites stoned achan and threw him into the fire, together with his family and all that they had. Then they raised over him a great heap of stones which is there to this day. For that reason, the place was called the valley of achor, which means misfortune. The lord's anger was assuaged, but, before the people dispersed, his stentorian voice rang out again, Be warned, he who offends me will pay, for I am the lord.

In order to take the city, joshua chose thirty thousand men of valour and instructed them as to the ambush they should prepare, a strategy that, this time, would meet with success, first, a ruse to divide the forces in the city and then an unstoppable attack on two fronts. Twelve thousand men and women died that day, the whole population of ai, for no one escaped and there was not one survivor. Joshua ordered the king of ai to be hanged from a tree until eventide. At sunset, he ordered his carcass to be taken down from the tree and deposited at the entrance to the city. They raised upon him a great heap of stones, which is also there to this day. Despite the many years that have passed, one might still perhaps find a few pebbles, one here, another over there, that will serve to confirm the truth of this regrettable story, drawn from very ancient documents. After what had just happened and remembering what had happened before, the destruction of sodom and gomorrah and the attack on jericho, cain made a decision and went to tell his boss, the farrier, I'm leaving, he said, I can't bear the sight of so many deaths, so much blood spilled, so much wailing and gnashing of teeth, give me back my donkey, I need him for the journey, You're making a mistake, from now on, the cities will fall one after the other, it will be more like a triumphal procession, and as for the donkey, if you were minded to sell him to me, I would be delighted to buy him, No, said cain, as I said, I need him, I wouldn't get very far on foot, What if I were to find you another one, for free, No, I came here with my donkey and I will leave with him, said cain, and putting his hand inside his tunic, he drew out a knife, I want that donkey now, this instant, otherwise, I'll kill you, But you would die too, We would both die, but you would die first, Wait for me here, I'll go and fetch him, said the farrier, Don't try any tricks on me, you know very well that you wouldn't come back alone, we'll both go, you and I, but remember, one wrong word from you and you'll feel this knife slip in between your ribs. The farrier was afraid that cain's anger might cause him to move from threat to deed, and it would be foolish to lose one's life over a donkey, however handsome a beast it might be. The two of them went together, they saddled up the donkey, cain was given some of the food being prepared for the soldiers, and when his saddlebags were good and full, he said to the farrier, Up you get, this will be your last ride on my donkey. Surprised, the man had no option but to obey, then cain jumped up behind him, and, in no time at all, they had left the encampment. Where are you taking me, asked the farrier anxiously, As I said, answered cain, for a ride. They rode and rode and when the tents were almost out of sight, cain said, Off you get. The farrier obeyed, but when he saw that cain was spurring the donkey on to continue his journey, he asked in alarm, What about me, what shall I do, Do what you like, but, if I were you, I'd go back to the encampment, It's a very long way, You won't get lost, just follow the columns of smoke that continue to rise from the city. And with that victory, cain's military career came to an end. He missed the conquest of the cities of makkedah, libnah, lachish, eglon, hebron and debir, where, once again, all the inhabitants were massacred, and to judge by the legend passed down from generation to generation until today, he also missed the greatest miracle of all times, when the lord made the sun stop so that joshua could win the battle, in daylight, against the five amorite kings. Apart from the inevitable and, by now, monotonous toll of deaths and casualties, apart from the usual destructions and even more usual fires, it's rather a fine story, illustrating the power of a god for whom, it would seem, nothing is impossible. All lies. The truth is that when joshua saw that the sun was going down and that the creeping shadows of the night would protect what remained of the amorite army, he raised his arms to heaven, with words ready prepared for posterity on his lips, but, at that moment, he heard a voice whisper in his ear, Silence, don't speak, say nothing, meet me alone, with no witnesses, in the tent of the ark of the covenant, we need to talk. Joshua obediently handed over operations to his second in command and hurried to the meeting place. He sat down on a stool and said, Here I am, lord, let me know thy will, You were probably thinking, said the lord, who was inside the ark, of asking me to stop the sun, Yes, lord, so that no amorite will escape us, Unfortunately, I cannot do as you ask. Joshua opened his mouth wide in amazement, You can't make the sun stop, he asked, and his voice trembled because he believed he was uttering a terrible heresy, No, I can't stop the sun because it's already stopped, it hasn't moved since I put it there, You are the lord, and therefore cannot be wrong, but that isn't what my eyes see, the sun is born over there, travels all day across the sky and disappears over the other side until it returns the following morning, Something moves, but it's not the sun, it's the earth, The earth doesn't move, lord, said joshua in a tense, desperate voice, Your eyes are deluding you, the earth does move, it turns on itself and also turns in space around the sun, In that case, order the earth to stop, it doesn't matter to me whether it's the sun that stops or the earth, just as long as I can destroy the amorites, If I were to stop the earth, not only the amorites would be destroyed, but the world itself, mankind, everything, all the creatures and every living thing on earth, even many trees, despite the roots that anchor them in the soil, everything would be hurled off like a stone from a sling, But I thought the workings of the world depended entirely on your will, lord, Yes, I've been using my will rather too much, as have others in my name, that's why there is so much discontent, people turning their backs on me, some even denying my existence, Punish them, They're beyond my jurisdiction, out of my control, the life of a god isn't as easy as you all think, a god cannot, as people imagine, simply say I want, I can and I command, and he can't always get what he wants straight away, but has to go round in circles first, it's true that I placed that mark on the forehead of cain, whom you've never seen and don't even know, but what I can't understand is why I don't have the power to stop him going where his will takes him and doing whatever he wishes, And what about us, now, asked joshua, his mind still fixed on the amorites, You will do exactly what you had already decided to do, I wouldn't want to take from you the glory of speaking directly to god, And what will you do, lord, Oh, I'll clear the sky of the clouds currently covering it, that's easy enough, but it's up to you to win the battle, With your encouragement, the battle will be over before the sun has set, Fine, given that I cannot do the impossible, I will do the possible. Interpreting these words as a dismissal, joshua got up from the stool, but the lord went on, Tell no one what has passed between us, the story that is told in the future should be ours and no other, joshua asked the lord to stop the sun and the lord did as he asked, that's all, My lips will remain sealed except to confirm that story, lord, Right, go and finish off those amorites for me. Joshua returned to the army, went up to the top of a hill and again raised his arms, O lord, he cried, lord of heaven, of the world and of israel, make the sun stand still in the west, so that your will can be done, give me one more hour of light, just one hour, so that the amorites cannot hide themselves like the cowards they are and so that your soldiers can find them in the darkness and administer your justice and take their lives. In reply, the voice of god thundered forth from the now cloudless sky, terrifying the amorites and emboldening the israelites, The sun will not move from where it is, in order to witness the battle of the israelites for the promised land, now, joshua, vanquish those five amorite kings defying me, and canaan will be the ripe fruit that will shortly fall into your hands, onwards then, and let no amorite survive the blade of the israelite sword. Some say that joshua's plea to the lord was simpler than that, more direct, that he said only, Sun, stand thou still upon gibeon, and thou, moon, in the valley of ajalon, which shows that joshua had accepted that he would have to fight after sunset and with only a pale moon to guide the points of sword and spear to the throats of the amorites. While this is an interesting version, it doesn't change the essence of the story, namely, that the amorites were roundly defeated and all credit for the victory went to the lord, who, having made the sun stop, did not need to wait for the moon. To every saint his candle, as is only right. Here is what was written in a book called just, whose whereabouts no one knows. The sun stood still in the midst of heaven, and hasted not to go down for about a whole day, and there was no day like that before it or after it, that the lord hearkened to the voice of a man, for the lord fought for israel.

10

Cain has no idea where he is, he can't tell if the donkey is taking him along one of the many roads of the past or along some narrow track in the future, or if, quite simply, he is trotting through some new present that has not, as yet, revealed itself. He looks at the parched earth, the thistles, the sparse scrub scorched by the sun, but parched earth, thistles and scrub are what one mainly sees in such barren places. There's not a road in sight, from here you could go anywhere or nowhere, as if the destinations were constantly shifting or had decided to wait for a better occasion to show themselves. The donkey is jogging steadily along, he seems to know where he's going, as if he were following a trail, or, rather, a confusing coming and going of tracks left by sandals, hooves or bare feet, that you have to study attentively if you want to avoid finding yourself going backwards when you thought you were heading straight for the north star. In the past, cain has been a would-be farmer, as well as a treader of clay, but he is now a diligent tracker, who, even at moments of uncertainty, tries not to lose the thread of those who have preceded him, regardless of whether or not they ever found a place where they could stop and say to themselves, I've arrived. Cain doubtless has very sharp eyes, but not so sharp that he can recognise his own marks among the many other tracks, the hollow left by his heel or the slightly scuffed print of his weary feet. Cain has passed this way before. He will realise this when he suddenly spots the remains of the ruined house where he once sheltered from the rain and where he will not be able to shelter today because what was left of the roof has fallen in, all one can see now are fragments of crumbling wall, which, after another two or three winters, will merge for ever with the earth from which they rose, earth to earth, dust to dust. From now on, the donkey will only go where he is told to, the days when he was the sole guide on this journey are over, or perhaps not, for left to his own devices, the memory of his former stable might be strong enough to lead him to the city that he left, who knows how many years before, carrying this man on his back. As for cain, he, naturally, has not forgotten the road to the palace. When he enters the palace, it will be in his power to change direction, to abandon the other presents awaiting him, both previous and future, and return to that familiar past for a day or two, possibly more, but not for all the remaining days of his life, for he has not yet met his fate, as we will see. Cain lightly touches the donkey's flanks with his heels, ahead lies the road that will lead him into the city, and there he will have no option but to drink whatever wine has been poured for him. Seen from close to, the city appears not to have grown, the same squat houses seemingly oppressed by their own weight, the same adobe bricks, only the palace rises above the dark mass of the older buildings, and, inevitably, in accordance with the rules of this story, just around the corner stands the same old man at the entrance to the square, leading the same sheep tethered by the same rope. Where have you been, have you come back to stay, he asked cain, And what about you, retorted cain, you're still here, are you, still not dead, As long as these sheep are alive, I will be too, I must have been born to tend them and stop them eating the rope that tethers them, There are worse fates, You mean your own, Maybe I'll tell you about that on another occasion, right now, I'm in a hurry, Is someone expecting you, asked the old man, That I don't know, Well, I'll just wait here to see if you leave or stay, Wish me luck, To do that I would need to know what is best for you, Even I don't know that, You're aware that lilith had a child, aren't you, asked the old man, Of course, she was pregnant when I left, Yes, well, she has a son, Goodbye, Goodbye. With no need to be told, the donkey headed for the palace gate, where he stopped. Cain slid down from the saddle, handed the reins to a slave who came to greet him and asked, Is anyone in the palace, Yes, my mistress is here, Go and tell her she has a visitor, Abel, your name is abel, murmured the slave, I remember you well, Off you go, then. The slave went up the steps and returned shortly afterwards, accompanied by a boy of about nine or ten, My son, thought cain. The slave beckoned cain to follow. At the top of the steps stood lilith, as beautiful and voluptuous as ever, I thought you would come today, that's why I put on this dress, to please you, Who is the boy, His name is enoch and he's your son. Cain went up the few steps that separated him from lilith, grasped the hands she held out to him and, in an instant, was holding her in his arms. He heard her sigh, felt her whole body tremble, and when lilith said, You came back, he could say only, Yes, I came back. At a signal from her, the slave led the boy away, leaving them alone. Come with me, she said. They went into the antechamber, and cain noticed that the guard's bed and bench that had been assigned to him ten years before were still there, How did you know I would come back today when I arrived here quite by chance, Never ask me how I know what I say I know because I won't be able to answer, but this morning, when I woke up, I said out loud, He will come back today, I said it so that you would hear, and it was true, here you are, but I won't ask you for how long, No, after all, I've only just arrived, it's hardly the time to speak of leaving, Why did you come back, That's a long story, too long to be told here, between rooms, Come and tell it to me in bed, then. They went into the bedroom, where nothing appeared to have changed, as if, during that long absence, cain's memory had been carefully modifying his recollections, one by one, so as not to feel surprised now. Lilith began to get undressed, and time seemed not to have passed for her at all. It was then that cain asked, What about noah, He died, she said, and her voice did not tremble nor did she look away, Did you kill him, asked cain, No, responded lilith, I promised you that I wouldn't, he died a natural death, Better so, said cain, The city is called enoch too, lilith remarked, Like my son, Yes, And who chose the name, Which name, The city's, Noah, And why did he name the city after a son that was not his, He never told me and I never asked, answered lilith, lying down. And when did noah die, asked cain, Three years ago, So for seven years, in the eyes of everyone, he was enoch's father, People pretended that was the case, but everyone here knew that you were the real father, although it's true that, over time, only the older people remembered, but be that as it may, noah could not have treated him better if he had been his own son, That doesn't sound like the man I knew, it's as if he were two people, No one is just one person, you, for example, are both cain and abel, And you, Oh, I am all women, and all their names are mine, said lilith, and now, be quick, come and give me news of your body, In ten years, I have known no other woman, said cain, as he lay down, And I have known no other man, said lilith, smiling mischievously, Is that true, No, there have been a few other men in this bed, but not many because, frankly, I couldn't stand them, I felt like slitting their throats when they ejaculated, Thank you for your honesty, To you I will never lie, said lilith and put her arms around him.

With their spirits soothed and their bodies amply compensated for that long separation, the moment arrived to put the past in order. Lilith had asked, Why did you come back, but he had already said that he didn't know how he had got there, and so she modified the question, What have you been doing all these years, and cain replied, I saw things that haven't yet happened, Do you mean you saw into the future, No, I was there, No one can be in the future, Then don't let's call it the future, let's call it another present or other presents, You've lost me, Yes, I found it hard to understand at first too, but then I realised that if I was there, and I really was, I must be in the present, a present, and what had been the future had ceased to be the future, tomorrow was now, No one's going to believe that, And I have no intention of telling anyone else, Your problem is that you have no proof, some object brought back from that other present, It wasn't just one present, but several, Give me an example. Then cain told lilith about the man called abraham whom the lord had commanded to sacrifice his own son, then about a great tower built by men who hoped to reach the sky and how the lord had razed it to the ground with a hurricane, then about the city where the men preferred to go to bed with other men and about the punishment of fire and brimstone that the lord caused to fall on them, with no thought for the children, who didn't even know what they might wish for in the future, and then about the vast throng of people at the foot of a mountain called sinai and the making of a golden calf, which those people worshipped and were slain for doing so, about the city that dared to kill thirty-six soldiers belonging to an army known as the israelites and whose population was wiped out down to the last child, and about another city, called jericho, whose walls were demolished by the blast from some trumpets made of rams' horns and then how everything inside it was destroyed, men and women, young and old, even oxen, sheep and asses. That is what I saw, concluded cain, and many more things for which I have no words, Do you really think that what you saw will happen in the future, asked lilith, Contrary to popular belief, the future is already written, it's just that we don't know how to read the page it's written on, said cain, wondering to himself where he had found such a revolutionary idea, And why do you think you were chosen to have that experience, Well, I'm not sure I was chosen, but I have learned one thing, What's that, That our god, the creator of heaven and earth, is completely mad, Do you dare to call the lord god mad, Only a madman unaware of what he was doing would admit to being directly responsible for the deaths of hundreds of thousands of people and then behave as if nothing had happened, unless, of course, it's not a case of real, authentic madness, but evil pure and simple, God could never be evil, if he was, he wouldn't be god, evil is what the devil is for, It can't be right for a god to order a father to kill his own son and burn him on a pyre simply as a test of faith, not even the wickedest of devils would order someone to do that, You've changed, you're not the same man who slept in this bed before, said lilith, You would not be the same woman if you had seen what I saw, the children of sodom burned to a cinder by the fires of heaven, Where's sodom, That's the city where the men preferred men to women, And was that why everyone was killed, Everyone, not a soul escaped, there were no survivors, Even the women whom those men spurned, lilith asked again, Even them, That's how it is with women, if the rain doesn't get you, the wind will, Anyway, the innocent are now accustomed to paying for the sinners, The lord seems to have a very strange idea of justice, Yes, the idea of someone who hasn't the slightest notion of what human justice might be,

Do you, asked lilith, I'm cain, remember, the one who killed his brother and was punished for his crime, Fairly leniently, it must be said, remarked lilith, Yes, you're right, I would be the first to admit that, but god, the one we call lord, was still the main person responsible, You wouldn't be here if you hadn't killed abel, in fact, from a selfish point of view, you could say that one thing led to the other, No, I just did what I had to do, killing my brother and sleeping with you in this bed are all effects of the same cause, Which cause, Being in god's hands, or in the hands of fate, to give him his other name, And what do you intend to do now, asked lilith, That depends, On what, Well, if I ever become master of my own life again, if this skipping from one present to another, completely independently of my will, ever stops, I will lead what is usually called a normal life, like everyone else, Not like everyone else, you will marry me, we already have a son, this is our city, and I will cling to you as faith-fully as the bark to its trunk, But if that doesn't happen, if my fate continues, then, wherever I am, I will be subject to being shunted from one present to another, and we will never be certain, you and I, what tomorrow might bring, besides, Besides what, asked lilith, It seems to me that what is happening must have some meaning, some significance, and I feel that I shouldn't stop halfway without trying to understand what it's about, So that means you won't be staying, that you'll leave again one day, said lilith, Yes, I think so, if I was born for something different, then I need to know what it is and why, Let's enjoy what time we have, then, come here, said lilith. They embraced and kissed, rolling from one side of the bed to the other, and when cain found himself on top of lilith and was about to penetrate her, she said, The mark on your forehead has grown bigger, Much bigger, asked cain, No, not very much, Sometimes I think it will grow and grow and spread all over my body and turn me into a negro, That's all I need, said lilith, laughing, a laugh that immediately became a groan of pleasure when, with one thrust, he drove his penis home.

Only two weeks later, cain disappeared. He had got into the habit of taking long walks on the outskirts of the city, not as before, because he was in need of sun and fresh air, natural benefits that had not been lacking in the last ten years, but to escape the oppressive atmosphere in the palace, where, apart from the hours spent in bed with lilith, he had nothing else to do, unless you count a few rather fruitless exchanges with the stranger that was enoch, his son.

11

Suddenly, he found himself going in through the gate of a city he had never visited before. His first thought was that he didn't have a penny on him and, as a stranger there, he could see no immediate way of earning one. If he had taken the donkey with him when he set out for his walk, this economic problem would have been easily resolved, because, as any buyer would have agreed, such a beast was worth his weight in gold. He asked two passers-by for the name of the city, and one of the men replied, This is the land of uz. The natural tone in which he said this, without a hint of impatience, encouraged cain to ask another question, And where might I find work, he asked, adding, as if to justify himself, I've only just arrived, you see, and I don't know anyone. The men looked him up and down and could see that he was neither a beggar nor a vagabond, although their eyes did linger a little longer on the mark on his forehead, and the second man said, The richest landowner in these parts and the greatest of all the men in the east is called job, you could try asking him for work, you might be lucky, And where would I find him, asked cain, Come with us, we'll take you there, he has so many servants that one more or less won't make any difference, Is he that rich, Immensely so, imagine being the owner of seven thousand sheep, three thousand camels, five hundred yoke of oxen and five hundred she-asses, The poor have a lot of imagination, said cain, indeed, you might say that's all they have, but I must confess I find such wealth unimaginable. There was a silence, and then one of the men remarked quite casually, We've met before, Yes, I have a vague recollection, said cain nervously, We angels have excellent memories, your name is cain and you were in sodom when the city was destroyed, Yes, that's true, I remember now, As you know, my colleague and I are angels of the lord, And what have I done to merit two angels of the lord helping me in my time of need, You were kind to abraham, you helped to ensure that no harm befell us in lot's house, and that deserves a reward, How can I thank you, We are angels, if we don't do good, who will, asked one. Cain took three deep breaths before summoning up the courage to ask, Given that your mission in sodom was to destroy the city, what mission brings you here, We cannot reveal that to anyone, said one, Well, it's not a secret exactly, said the other, and it won't be a secret once things start to happen, besides, this man has shown he can be trusted, Well, it's up to you, but what if he runs and tells job, Job probably wouldn't believe him, Fine, do as you please, I wash my hands of it. Cain stopped and said, Please don't fall out because of me, tell me if you want, but if you don't, don't, it really doesn't matter either way. In the face of such selflessness, the more reticent of the angels gave in, Go on, he said, tell him, then fixing cain with a stern eye, he said,

But you must swear that you will reveal to no one else what you are about to hear, I swear, declared cain, raising his right hand. The other angel said, A few days ago, as happens now and then, all the celestial beings were gathered before god, including satan, and god asked him, Where have you been, and satan answered, I have been walking to and fro about the earth, Did you notice my servant job, there is none like him on the earth, he is a perfect and upright man, who fears god and eschews evil. Satan, who listened to these words with a scornful sneer on his face, asked the lord, Do you really think his religious feelings are entirely disinterested, isn't it true that, like a hedge, you protect him on all sides, him and his family and everything that belongs to him. He paused, then went on, But if you were to put forth your hand and touch what is his, you would see how he would curse you. Then the lord said to satan, Everything he has is at your disposal, but him you cannot touch. When satan heard this, he left, which is why we are here, To do what, asked cain, To make sure that satan doesn't go too far, that he doesn't overstep the mark the lord has set him. Then cain said, If I've understood you rightly, the lord and satan made a wager, but this man job isn't to know that he is the object of that gamblers' agreement between god and the devil, Exactly, exclaimed the angels as one, That doesn't seem very fair of the lord, said cain, if it's true, as I've heard, that job, for all his wealth, is also a good and upright man, and very religious too, he has committed no crime, and yet, for no reason, he is about to be punished with the loss of all his money and possessions, now it may be, as many people say, that the lord is just, but I don't think so, it reminds me of what happened to abraham, whom god, in order to put him to the test, commanded to kill his son isaac, it seems to me that if the lord doesn't trust the people who believe in him, I really don't see why those people should trust in the lord, The ways of the lord are inscrutable, not even we angels can fathom the workings of his mind, Oh, I've had enough of all this nonsense about the lord's ways being inscrutable, answered cain, god should be as clear and transparent as a pane of glass and not go wasting his energies on creating an atmosphere of constant terror and fear, god, in short, does not love us, He it was who gave you life, My father and mother gave me life, they joined flesh to flesh and I was born, there's no evidence that god was present at the act, God is everywhere, Especially when it comes to ordering people to be killed, why, the death of just one of the children burned to death in sodom would be enough to condemn him outright, but for god, justice is an empty word, and now he's going to make job suffer because of a bet and no one will hold him to account, Be careful, cain, you're talking too much, the lord is listening and, sooner or later, he will punish you, The lord isn't listening, he's deaf, everywhere the poor, unfortunate and wretched cry out to him for help, they plead with him for some remedy that the world denies them, and the lord turns his back on them, he started out by making a pact with the hebrews and now here he is making a pact with the devil, what's the point of having a god. The angels protested indignantly and threatened to leave him there with no work, but at that point, the theological debate ended, and the three men more or less made their peace. One of the angels even said, I think the lord would enjoy discussing these matters with you, One day perhaps, said cain. They were standing at the door of job's mansion, and one of the angels asked to speak to the steward, who did not come in person, but sent a representative to find out what they wanted, Work, said the angel, not for us, because we are not from around here, but for our friend who has just arrived and wants to start a new life in the land of uz, What can you do, asked the under-steward, Well, I know a little about donkeys, I was assistant to the farrier in joshua's army, Very good, that's an excellent recommendation, I will send a slave with you and you can start work at once, I just need to know your name, Cain, And where are you from, From the land of nod, Hm, I've never heard of the place, You're not the first, saying the land of nod is tantamount to saying the land of nowhere. Then one of the angels said to cain, There you are, now you have work, For as long as it lasts, replied cain, with a glum smile, Don't be so pessimistic, said the under-steward, anyone fortunate enough to enter this house will have work for life, there's no better man than job. The angels said goodbye and embraced cain before returning to their task of ensuring that the lord's orders were carried out, besides, who knows, it may all turn out better than we think.

Unfortunately, it turned out far worse than could ever have been expected. Armed with the carte blanche given to him by the lord, satan attacked simultaneously on all fronts. One day, while job's sons and daughters, seven sons and three daughters, were eating and drinking wine in the eldest brother's house, a messenger came to job's house, our very own cain, who, as we know, had been employed to tend the she-asses, and he said to job, The oxen were ploughing and the asses feeding beside them, when the sabeans fell upon them and took them away and put all the servants to the sword, and only I escaped alone to tell you. Cain was still speaking when another messenger arrived, The fire of god is fallen from heaven and has burned up the sheep and the slaves and only I escaped alone to tell you. While he was still speaking, there came another, The chaldeans, he said, divided into three groups and fell upon the camels and carried them off, having first put the servants to the sword, and only I escaped alone to tell you. While he was still speaking, there came another, who said, Your sons and your daughters were eating and drinking wine in the eldest brother's house, when suddenly the came a great wind from the wilderness and smote the four corners of the house and it fell in upon them and killed them, and only I escaped alone to tell you. Then job stood up and rent his cloak and shaved his head, and fell down upon the ground and said, Naked came I out of my mother's womb and naked shall I return to the womb of the earth, the lord gave and the lord has taken away, blessed be the name of the lord. The disasters befalling this unfortunate family will not stop here, but before proceeding, allow us a few remarks. The first is to express our bewilderment at the fact that satan was able to do as he pleased with the sabeans and the chaldeans in order to serve his particular interests, the second is to express our even greater bewilderment on learning that satan had been authorised to make use of a natural phenomenon, in this case a great wind, and worse still, and this really is inexplicable, to use god's own fire to burn the sheep and the slaves tending them. So, either satan is far more powerful than we thought, or what we are seeing here is a grave case of tacit complicity, assuming it was tacit, between good and evil. Mourning had fallen like a tombstone on the land of uz, because all those who died had been born in the city, which was now condemned, who knows for how long, to a general poverty in which job would not be the least of the poor. A few days after these unhappy events, there was another gathering of the celestial beings, and satan was again amongst them. The lord asked him, Where have you been, and satan answered, I have been going to and fro on the earth and walking up and down in it, Did you notice my servant job, asked the lord, there is none like him on the earth, he is a perfect and upright man, who fears god and eschews evil, and who still holds fast to his integrity, even though you moved me to destroy him for no reason, and satan answered, I did so with your agreement, whether or not job deserved it was none of my business, neither was the idea of tormenting him, and he went on, A man is capable of giving all that he has to save his life, even his own skin, but put forth your hand now and make him suffer illness in his own bones and body and you will see that he will curse you to your face. The lord said, He is in your hands, but on condition that you spare his life, That is all I require, answered satan and he left the gathering to go and find job and, before you

119

could say knife, he had covered him with boils from the soles of his feet to the crown of his head. It was terrible to see the poor man sitting in the dust of the road while he scraped the pus from his legs with a potsherd, like the lowest of the low. Job's wife, who had not said a word until now, not even to mourn the death of her ten children, felt that it was time to speak up and she asked her husband, Do you still cling to your integrity, if I were you, if I were in your place, I would curse god even if, by doing so, I risked bringing about my own death, to which job responded, You speak like a foolish woman, if we receive good from god, why should we not also receive evil, that was his question, but his wife answered angrily, Evil is satan's business, it would never have occurred to me that god would appear to us now in the guise of satan's rival, God cannot have put me in this state, only satan, Yes, but with the lord's agreement, she said, adding, According to the ancients, the devil's wiles would never prevail over the will of god, but I'm not sure now that things are that simple, it seems likely that satan is just another instrument of the lord, the one who does the dirty work to which god prefers not to put his name. Then job, at the height of his suffering, and perhaps, although without admitting as much, encouraged by his wife, broke the dyke of the fear of god sealing his lips and cried, Let the day perish wherein I was born, and the night in which it was said, There is a man-child conceived, let that day be darkness, let not god regard it from above, neither let the light shine upon it, let darkness and the shadow of death stain it, let a cloud dwell upon it, let the blackness

120

of the day terrify it, let it not be joined to the other days of the year, let it not be counted among the months, let that night be solitary, let no joyful voice come therein, let the stars of the twilight be dark, let it look for light, but have none, neither let it see the dawning of the day, because it shut not up the doors of my mother's womb nor hid sorrow from me, thus job bemoaned his fate, pages and pages of imprecations and lamentations, while three friends of his, eliphaz the temanite, bildad the shuhite and zophar the naamathite lectured him on the need for resignation and on the duty of all believers to bow their head to the will of god whatever that will might be. Cain had managed to find employment, the fairly lowly task of looking after the donkeys of a small landowner, to whom he had to repeat over and over, to him and his relatives, the story of the attack by the sabeans and their theft of the she-asses. He reckoned that the angels must still be around, collecting information about job's misfortunes in order to carry the news back to the lord, who would be impatient to hear them, but, to his surprise, they were the ones who sought him out, to congratulate him on having escaped the cruelty of the sabean nomads, A miracle, they said. Cain, of course, thanked them, but that prerogative did not make him forget his grievances with god, which were growing steadily, The lord must be very happy, he said to the angels, he won his bet against satan, and despite all job's sufferings, he has still not denied god, We knew he wouldn't, And god knew too, I imagine, Oh yes, the lord most of all, Which means that he made the wager because he knew he would win, In a way, yes, So nothing has changed, then, the lord knows no more about job than he did before, True, In that case, can you explain to me why job should have been transformed into a leper, covered in suppurating wounds, having lost all his children and all his wealth, The lord will find some way of compensating him, Will he resuscitate his ten children, raise the walls of his house and bring back the animals that were killed, asked cain, That we don't know, And what will the lord do to satan, who would seem to have abused the authority given to him, Probably nothing, Nothing, asked cain, scandalised, slaves may not count in the statistics, but a lot of other people died too, and you're telling me that the lord will probably do nothing, It's not our fault, that's how it's always been in heaven, The fact that satan should be present at a gathering of celestial beings is, in itself, incomprehensible to any mere mortal. The conversation ended there, the angels left, and cain began to think that he really should find a more dignified path in life, I'm not going to stay here for ever, looking after donkeys, he thought. This praiseworthy notion was deserving of consideration, but, unfortunately, his options were nil, apart from going back to the land of nod and taking his place at the palace and in lilith's bed. He would grow fat there and give her two or three more children, but now another idea occurred to him, that of going to see how his parents were, to find out if they were still alive and if they were all right. He would wear a disguise so as to go unrecognised, but no one would deprive him of that joy. Joy, he asked himself, for cain there can never be any joy, cain is the man who killed his brother, cain is the man born to witness the unspeakable, cain is the man who hates god.

However, he needed a donkey to take him there. At first, he even considered forgetting about donkeys altogether and travelling on foot, but if it took a long time before he was sent to another present, he would have no option but to wander those deserts, guiding himself by the stars at night and, by day, waiting for them to come out. Besides, he would have no one to talk to. Contrary to what most people think, the donkey is a great conversationalist, one need think only of its many ways of braying and snorting and the sheer variety of its ear movements, however, not everyone who rides a donkey knows that language, which is why seemingly inexplicable situations arise, like when the creature stops in the middle of the road, motionless, and refuses to budge even if beaten. People say then that the donkey is as stubborn as a mule, when, in fact, it's simply a communication problem, as happens so often between human beings. The idea of travelling on foot did not, therefore, last long in cain's mind. He needed a donkey, even if he had to steal one, but we, who are gradually getting to know him better, also know that he will not do this. Cain may be a murderer, but he's an essentially honest man, and even the dissolute days he spent in concubinal bliss with lilith, however reprehensible in bourgeois eyes, were not enough to alter his innate moral sense, one has only to think of the way he bravely stands up to god, although, truth be told, the lord has not as yet noticed, unless one recalls the discussion they had over abel's still-warm body. In this toing and froing of thoughts, cain had the providential idea of buying one of the donkeys in his care, by taking only half his salary and leaving the other half in the hands of the landowner as payment on account. It would take a long time to pay off this debt, but cain was in no hurry, no one in the world was expecting him, not even lilith, however nervously and impatiently her body might toss and turn in bed. The owner of the donkeys, who was a decent man, drew up the accounts in his own fashion and to cain's benefit, not that cain noticed, mathematics never having been his strong point. It did not take many weeks before cain found himself, at last, in possession of his own donkey. He could leave when he wished. On the eve of his departure, he decided to go and see how his previous employer was doing, to see if the sores left by the boils had now healed, but was horrified to find him still sitting on the ground at the door of his house, scraping at the wounds on his leg with a potsherd, just as he had been on the day when the curse fell upon him, for god's surrender of him into satan's hands had proved to be the very worst of curses. Much coin, much care, people say, and job's story demonstrates that to the full. Discreet as any fugitive has to be, cain did not approach job to wish him some improvement in his health, after all, employer and employee had never met, that's the problem with social divisions, with each of us stuck in our own place, preferably the place we were born, how then will we ever make friendships with people from different worlds. Mounted on the donkey that now belongs to him by right, cain returned to his place of work to prepare what he needed for the journey. In comparison with the donkey he had left behind in lilith's stables at the palace, the magnificent beast that had prompted the envy of the farrier at jericho, this new mount is more of a retired rocinante than an animal to be led proudly out on parades. However, even the least demanding of independent minds will acknowledge that the beast has good strong legs, albeit somewhat skinny and inelegant. All in all, cain is not ill served, thought the donkey's former owner, who came to the door to say goodbye when cain, early the following morning, finally set off.

12

He didn't have to travel very far to leave behind him the sad present of the land of uz and find himself, instead, surrounded by green mountains and lush valleys flowing with streams of such pure, crystalline water as eye had never seen nor mouth tasted. It could have been the garden of eden of now fond memory, for the passing years had taken with them many a painful recollection. And yet, there was something false and artificial about that dazzling landscape, as if it were a backdrop specially prepared for some purpose quite indecipherable to someone riding a very ordinary donkey and without a michelin guide to hand. Cain rode past a large outcrop of rock that concealed a broad section of the panorama and emerged on the other side at the entrance to another valley, less verdant perhaps, but no less attractive than those seen earlier, and there he saw a wooden construction, which, given the shape of its component parts and the colour of the materials it was made from, looked very like a boat, or, to be more exact, a huge ark whose presence there was all the more intriguing, because a boat, if it was a boat, is usually built near water, and an ark, certainly one of that size, isn't something one would leave in a valley, waiting for who knows what. Curious, cain decided to seek out a reliable source of information, in this case, the people building that enigmatic boat or no less enigmatic ark, either for their own use or under orders from someone else. He made his way with the donkey down to the shipyard, where he greeted those present and tried to strike up a conversation, Beautiful place this, he said, but the reply, as well as being a long time in coming, was given as succinctly as possible, a merely confirmatory, indifferent, impartial, non-committal yes. Cain went on, A grand construction like this is the very last thing any traveller, myself, for example, would expect to come across, but this intentionally flattering hint went unheeded. It was clear that the eight workers, four men and four women, had no desire to fraternise with the intruder and made no attempt to disguise the wall of hostility with which they defended themselves against his advances. Cain decided to stop beating about the bush and come straight to the point, So what are you making, what is it, a boat, an ark, a house, he asked. The oldest member of the group, a tall man, as strong as samson, said only, It's not a house, And it's not an ark either, said cain, because arks always have lids, and if this thing had a lid, no amount of human strength could lift it. The man did not respond and made as if to move away, but cain stopped him at the last moment, If it isn't a house and it isn't an ark, then it must be a boat, he said, Don't answer him, noah, said the older of the four women, the lord will be angry with you if you talk too much. The man nodded and said to cain, We have a lot to do and you're distracting us from our work, please leave us alone and go on your way, adding in a slightly threatening tone, As you can see, there are four strong men here, myself and my sons, Fine, replied cain, it would seem that the old rules of mesopotamian hospitality, which have always been respected in our land, have lost all value for the family of noah. At that precise moment, the lord appeared, with a deafening roll of thunder and accompanying pyrotechnics. He was wearing his work clothes, rather than the usual luxurious vestments that he could always rely on to reduce those whom he wanted to impress to immediate obedience without having to resort to divine dialectic. Noah and his family immediately prostrated themselves on the ground, which was covered in wood shavings, while the lord looked at cain in some surprise and asked, What are you doing here, I haven't seen you since the day you killed your brother, That's where you're wrong, lord, we did see each other, only you didn't recognise me, in abraham's tent by the oaks of mamre, before you destroyed sodom, An excellent piece of work that, clean and efficient, and more importantly, definitive, There's nothing definitive in the world you created, poor job thought he was safe from all misfortunes, but your wager with satan brought him poverty and made of his body a running sore, at least that was how he was when I left the land of uz, Not any more, cain, not any more, his skin has healed completely and his herds and flocks have doubled, now he has fourteen thousand sheep, six thousand camels, a thousand yoke of oxen and a thousand asses, And how did he manage that, He bowed to my authority, he recognised that my power is absolute, limitless, that the only person I have to account to is myself, that I never have to concern myself with considerations of a personal nature, and that I am endowed, let me say this to you now, with a conscience so flexible that it agrees with whatever I do, And what about job's children, who died beneath the rubble of a house, A minor detail of little importance, he'll have another ten children, seven boys and three girls, to replace the ten he lost, Just like the animals, Exactly, after all, children are the same as flocks, nothing more. Noah and his family had got up from the ground now and were listening in astonishment to the dialogue between the lord and cain, which resembled that of two old friends meeting again after a long separation. You haven't told me what you came here to do, Oh, nothing special, lord, besides, I didn't come here, I found myself here, Just as you found yourself in sodom and in the land of uz, And at mount sinai, and in jericho, and at the tower of babel and in the land of nod, and at the sacrifice of isaac, You've done a lot of travelling, Indeed, lord, but it was not of my own choosing, I even wondered if these constant changes that have taken me from one present to another, now in the past, now in the future, were not your work too, No, it's nothing to do with me, such primitive skills, such tricks intended to épater le bourgeois, are beyond me, time does not exist for me, So you admit, then, that there is another force in the universe, different from and more powerful than yours, It's possible, but I'm not in the habit of indulging in such idle speculations, one thing is certain, though, you cannot leave this valley, and I would advise you not to try, from now on, each exit will be guarded by two cherubim bearing flaming swords and with orders to kill anyone who approaches, Like the angel you placed at the gates of eden, How do you know about that, My parents often spoke about him. God turned to noah and asked, Have you told this man what the boat is for, No, lord, may my tongue fall from my mouth if I lie, my family are my witnesses, You are a loyal servant, I did well to choose you, Thank you, lord, now, if you don't mind my asking, what should I do with this man, Take him with you on the boat and make him one of your family, that way you will have another man to give your daughters-in-law babies, their husbands won't mind, I hope, They won't, I promise, and I will do my best as well, for old as I am, I'm not so old as to turn up my nose at a good-looking woman. Cain decided to intervene, Would you mind telling me what you're talking about, he asked, and the lord responded as if repeating a speech he had given before and knew by heart, The earth is corrupt and filled with violence, I find in it only corruption, for all its inhabitants have strayed from the path, the wickedness of man is great, every thought and desire incline always and constantly towards evil, I repent ever having created man, for he has grieved me to the heart, the end of all flesh is come before me, for the earth is filled with violence through them, I will destroy them along with the earth, I have chosen you, noah, to start a new race, which is why I have ordered you to build an ark of gopher wood, and to make rooms in the ark, and to cover it inside and out with pitch, I commanded you to make it three hundred cubits long, fifty cubits in breadth, and thirty cubits high and to make a window for the ark, and finish it to a cubit above, and to set the door of the ark in its side, and to make it with lower, second, and third decks, for I am going to bring a flood of waters upon the earth to destroy all flesh in which there is the breath of life under heaven, everything that is on the earth will die, but I will establish my covenant with you, noah, and you shall come into the ark, you, your sons, your wife and your sons' wives with you, and of every living thing of all flesh, you shall bring two of every sort into the ark to keep them alive with you, male and female, be they birds, quadrupeds or other animals, you must also take with you the different kinds of food eaten by each species, and store it up to serve as provisions for you and for them. This was the lord's speech. Then cain said, A vessel of that size and so heavily laden will never float, when the valley begins to flood, no amount of water will be enough to lift the ark off the ground, everyone will drown and the hoped-for salvation will turn out to have been a mousetrap, Not according to my calculations, said the lord, Your calculations are wrong, a boat should be built next to water, not in a valley surrounded by mountains at a vast distance from the sea, normally, when you finish building a boat, you carry it down to the water, and it's the sea itself or the river, if you're by a river, that lifts the boat, you don't seem to realise that the reason a boat floats is because any object partially or wholly submerged in a fluid experiences an upward impulse equal to the weight of the volume of fluid dislodged, it's the archimedes principle, May I give my opinion, lord, asked noah, Speak, said god, who was clearly much put out, Cain is right, lord, if we wait here for the water to lift us, we will all end up drowned and there will be no new human race. Furrowing his brow in thought, the lord considered the matter and finally came to the same conclusion, all that work to invent a valley that had never existed before, and for nothing. Then he said, I have a solution, when the ark is ready, I will send my worker angels to carry it through the air to the nearest bit of sea, It's very heavy, lord, the angels won't be able to lift it, You don't know how strong my angels are, they can lift a mountain on one finger, fortunately, they're highly disciplined, otherwise they might easily have organised a plot to depose me, Like satan, said cain, Yes, like satan, but I've found a way of keeping him sweet, I give him a victim to amuse himself with now and then, and that seems to satisfy him, Just as you did with job, who didn't dare to curse you, but who carries all the bitterness of the world in his heart, What do you know of job's heart, Nothing, but I know all about mine and a little about yours, retorted cain, Oh, I doubt that, we gods are like bottomless wells, if you lean over us, you won't even see your own image reflected back, Eventually, all wells dry up, and your hour will come as well. The lord did not reply to this, but he looked very hard at cain and said, That mark on your forehead has grown bigger, it looks like a black sun rising up above the horizon of your eyes, Bravo, cried cain, applauding, I had no idea you went in for poetry, There, you see, you know absolutely nothing about me. With this aggrieved comment, god departed far more discreetly than he had arrived, by simply vanishing into another dimension.

Prompted by a discussion in which, in the opinion of any impartial observer, he had not cut the finest of figures, the lord decided to change his plan. Destroying humanity wasn't what you could call an urgent task, the inevitable extinction of that man-beast could wait another two or three or even ten centuries, but having made the decision, he felt a kind of tingling in his fingertips, which was a sign of grave impatience. He decided, therefore, to mobilise his legion of worker angels with immediate effect, and instead of just using them to carry the ark to the sea as he had now decided to do, he ordered them to help noah's exhausted family whose labours, as anyone could see, had left them more dead than alive. A few days later, the angels arrived, in ranks of three, and set to work at once. The lord was not exaggerating when he boasted about how strong his angels were, you only had to see how easily they picked up a thick plank under one arm, as if it were the evening paper, and carried it, if necessary, from one end of the ark to the other, three hundred cubits or, in modern measurements, nearly five hundred feet, almost the length of an aircraft carrier. The most surprising thing, though, was the way in which they hammered the nails into the wood. They didn't use a hammer, they simply put the nail in place, point downwards, and hit the head hard with their fist, and the nail would slide easily in, as if the extremely hard wood were butter in summer. Watching them plane a plank was even more amazing, they would simply run the palm of their hand back and forth, without producing any shavings or even a hint of sawdust, until the plank was the desired thickness. And if they had to make a hole for a dowel, they just used their forefinger. It was a real experience watching them work. It's hardly surprising, therefore, that the work advanced with previously unimaginable speed, so fast that there was scarcely time to appreciate the changes. During this period, the lord appeared only once. He asked noah how things were progressing and enquired as to whether cain was helping the family, oh, indeed he was, he had already slept with two of the daughters-in-law and was preparing to sleep with the third. The lord also asked if he was managing to gather together the animals who would be travelling with them in the ark, and noah told him that most had been found and that, as soon as the ark was finished, they would find those that were still missing. This was only a very small part of the truth. There were some animals, the most common ones, kept in a paddock at the far end of the valley, but they were a tiny fraction of those envisaged by the plan set out by the lord, namely, every living thing of all flesh, from the pot-bellied hippopotamus to the most insignificant of fleas, not forgetting the even smaller creatures, all the way down to microorganisms, who are also flesh. In the same ample, generous interpretation of the word flesh, there are also those creatures widely spoken of in certain exclusive, esoteric circles, but whom no one can claim to have seen. We are referring, for example, to the unicorn, the phoenix, the hippogryph, the centaur, the minotaur, the basilisk, the chimera, and that whole prodigious, composite class of animals with only one justification for their existence, that of having been created by god in a moment of extravagance, as was the common-or-garden donkey, with whom these lands are teeming. Imagine the pride, the prestige, the respect noah would gain in the eyes of the lord if he could persuade just one of those animals to enter the ark, preferably the unicorn, always supposing he could find one. The problem with the unicorn is that there are no females, and so it cannot reproduce via the normal routes of fecundation and gestation, although, on second thoughts, perhaps that isn't necessary, after all, biological continuity isn't everything, it's enough that the human mind can create and recreate whatever creature it obscurely believes in. For the remaining tasks, gathering together the animals and the necessary food supplies, for example, noah is hoping to be able to rely on the efficient help of the worker angels, who, all honour to them, continue to work with praiseworthy enthusiasm. Among themselves, the angels were happy to acknowledge that life in heaven was the most boring thing ever invented, with the chorus of angels constantly proclaiming to the four winds the lord's greatness, generosity and even his beauty. It's high time that these and other angels began to experience the simple joys of ordinary people, it shouldn't always be necessary, in order to generate a little excitement, to rain down fire on sodom or to sound their trumpets and bring down the walls of jericho. In this case, at least from the point of view of the worker angels, happiness on earth was far superior to that in heaven, but the lord, of course, being a jealous god, must never know this, because if he did, such seditious thoughts

135

would merit the severest of reprisals with no regard for the perpetrators' angelic status. Thanks to the harmonious atmosphere that reigned among the people working on the ark, cain, when the time came, was able to get his donkey on board, as a stowaway, thus saving him from the general drowning. It was also thanks to this cordial relationship that he became privy to the angels' doubts and perplexities. Cain asked two of the angels, with whom he had established what, in human terms, would be described as bonds of camaraderie and friendship, if they really thought that, once this humanity had been destroyed, the race that followed would not fall into the same errors, the same temptations, the same follies and crimes, and they answered, We are mere angels, we know little about this incomprehensible charade that you call human nature, but to be perfectly frank, we don't see how the second experiment will be any more satis-factory than the first, which ended in the long string of miseries we see before us now, in short, in our honest opinion as angels, and considering all the evidence, we don't believe that human beings deserve life, Do you really believe that man doesn't deserve to live, asked cain, shocked, That isn't what we said, what we said, and we repeat, is that given the behaviour of human beings through the ages, they do not deserve life, with its many dark sides, in all its beauty, grandeur and magnificence, replied one of the angels, So saying one thing is not the same as saying the other, added the second angel, It may not be the same, but it almost is, But the difference lies in that almost, and that difference is enormous, As far as I know, we men never ask ourselves

136

whether or not we deserve life, said cain, If you had, perhaps you wouldn't be about to vanish from the face of the earth, Well, there's no point crying about it now, said cain, giving voice to the sombre pessimism acquired during his successive journeys into the horrors of past and future, if the children who were burned to death in sodom hadn't been born, they wouldn't have had to scream the screams I heard while fire and brimstone fell from the heavens on to their innocent heads, That was their parents' fault, said one of the angels, There was no reason why the children should suffer because of that, Your mistake is to assume that guilt is understood in the same way by god and by men, said one of the angels, In the case of sodom, the guilt lies with a god who was in such a ridiculous hurry that he didn't want to waste time selecting for punishment only those who, in his eyes, were the evil-doers, besides, where did the strange idea come from, that god, simply because he is god, has the right to govern the private lives of his believers, setting up rules, prohibitions, interdictions and other such nonsense, asked cain, We don't know, said one of the angels, We're told almost nothing about such things, we're only called in to do the heavy work, added the other in a tone of complaint, when the time comes to lift the boat and carry it to the sea, you can be quite sure that there will be no seraphim, cherubim, thrones or archangels around, That doesn't surprise me, cain started to say, but the words were left hanging in the air, suspended, while a kind of wind beat in his ears and he suddenly found himself inside a tent. A naked man was lying on the ground, and that man was noah who was plunged in the deepest of drunken sleeps. Another man was having carnal relations with him, and that man was ham, his youngest son, who was, in turn, the father of canaan. Ham saw his father naked, which was an elliptical, rather discreet way of describing the embarrassing or reprehensible thing that was actually happening. Worse still was the fact that the guilty son then went and told shem and japheth, who were standing outside the tent, but they compassionately took a blanket and, walking backwards, so that they would not see their father's nakedness, covered him over. When noah wakes up and realises the shame ham has brought on him, he will let fall upon his son the curse that will harm all the people of canaan, Cursed be canaan, he will be the servant of servants to his brothers, and blessed be shem by the lord god and let canaan be his servant, may god enlarge japheth and he shall dwell in the tents of shem and let canaan be his servant. Cain, however, will no longer be there, the same gust of wind brought him back to the door of the ark just as noah and his son ham were approaching with the latest news, We leave tomorrow, they said, the animals are all in the ark, the foodstuffs are safely stowed, we can weigh anchor.

13

God was not there for the launch. He was busy examining the planet's hydraulic system, checking the state of the valves, tightening the odd loose screw that was dripping where it shouldn't, testing the various local distribution networks, keeping an eye on the manometers, as well as dealing with tens of myriads of other tasks, large and small, each of them more important than the last, and which only he, as creator, engineer and administrator of the universal mechanisms, was in a position to carry out and to which only he could give the sacred ok. Parties were for other people, he had work to do. At such times, he felt less like a god and more like the foreman of the worker angels, who, at that precise moment, were waiting in their immaculately white overalls, one hundred and fifty on the starboard of the ark and one hundred and fifty on the port side, for the order to lift the enormous vessel, but we could not say that an order rang out, because no voice would be heard, for this operation is all in the mind, in one mind, as if only one man with a single brain and a single will were thinking it. One moment the ark was on the ground, the next it had been lifted chest-high by the worker angels, as if they were performing an exercise with weights and dumb-bells. Noah and his family leaned excitedly out of the window the better to appreciate the spectacle, at the risk, thought cain, of one of them falling out. One last push and the ark was suddenly raised into the upper air. It was then that noah shouted, The unicorn, the unicorn. And indeed, galloping alongside the ark was that creature without equal in zoology, with its spiral horn, its dazzling white coat, like an angel, that mythical horse whose existence so many had doubted, and there it was, almost within their grasp, all they had to do was lower the ark, open the door and lure it in with a lump of sugar, which is the favourite treat of all equines, and can be their perdition. Suddenly, the unicorn disappeared as quickly as it had appeared. Noah's cries of, Go down, go down, were all in vain. Manoeuvring the ark earthwards again would have been very complicated logistically, and what was the point if the unicorn had vanished and would now be wandering who knows where. Meanwhile, at a far greater speed than that of the hindenburg airship, the ark was cutting through the air, heading for the sea, where, when the water was deemed deep enough, it finally landed, creating a huge wave as it did so, a real tsunami, that raced up the beaches, destroying the boats and huts of fishermen, drowning quite a few and ruining the local fishing industry, like a warning of things to come. The lord, however, did not change his mind, his calculations might be wrong, but as long as no one else had checked them, he still had the benefit of the doubt. Inside the ark, noah's family was giving thanks to god, and to celebrate the success of the operation and show their gratitude, they sacrificed a lamb to the lord, who was delighted, as is only natural, given where the lamb had come from. The lord was right, noah had been an excellent choice as father of the new human race, for as the only just and honest person of his day, he would correct the errors of the past and drive iniquity from the earth. And the angels, where are the worker angels, asked cain suddenly. They were not there. Having carried out the lord's commands so perfectly and completely, those diligent workers, with characteristic simplicity, as we saw on the very first day we met them, had returned to barracks with no expectation of any medals being handed out. It is as well to remember that the ark has neither rudder nor sail, it has no motor, you can't wind it up, and resorting to oars would be simply unthinkable, not even the strength of all the worker angels in heaven would be capable of such a feat. It will move, therefore, at the whim of the currents, it will be pushed by the winds that blow the belly of the ship along, there will be very little sailing skill involved and the journey will be one long rest, apart from bouts of amatory activity, which will be neither few and far between nor brief, and to which cain's contribution, as far as we can ascertain, has been exemplary. Just ask noah's daughters-in-law, who have frequently left their beds in the middle of the night, where they have been lying with their husbands, in order to go and cover themselves, not just with the blanket covering cain, but with his young, experienced body.

141

After seven days had passed, seven being a kabbalistic number par excellence, the floodgates of heaven opened. The rain will fall unceasingly upon the earth for forty days and forty nights. At first, the cataracts falling continuously from the sky with a deafening roar appeared to make little difference. That was only natural, the force of gravity guided the torrents into the sea, into which they appeared to vanish, but it was not long before the fountains of the ocean deeps overflowed too and the water began to rise to the surface in gushes and spouts as high as mountains that came and went, merging with the vastness of the sea. In the midst of these wild aquatic convulsions that seemed bent on swallowing everything, the boat managed to survive, bobbing about like a cork, always righting itself at the last moment, just when the sea seemed about to gulp it down. After one hundred and fifty days, once the fountains of the deep and the floodgates of the heavens had closed, the water, which had covered even the highest of mountains, began slowly to subside. Meanwhile, though, one of noah's daughters-in-law, ham's wife, had died in an accident. Contrary to what we said or implied earlier, there was a great need for manpower on board, not sailors, it's true, but cleaners. Hundreds, not to say thousands, of animals, many of them very large indeed, were crammed into the hold, shitting and peeing for all they were worth. Cleaning this up, shovelling tons of excrement into buckets every day was a terrible burden for the four women, both physically, because they were totally exhausted, poor things, but also sensorially, with the unbearable stink of shit and urine that seemed to penetrate their very skin. On one of those days of tumultuous tempests, with the ark being shaken by the storm and the animals trampling each other, ham's wife slipped on the filthy deck and ended up beneath the feet of an elephant. The others threw her into the sea just as they found her, all bloody and smeared with excrement, like a miserable bit of human detritus without honour or dignity. Why didn't you clean her up first, asked cain, and noah replied, There'll be water enough in the sea to wash her clean. From that moment on and until the end of the story, cain would feel a deep-seated loathing for noah. They say that there is no effect without cause and no cause without effect, and that would seem to indicate that the relationship between the two things should, at every moment, be not only obvious but graspable in every aspect, whether consequent or subsequent. We would not, however, go so far as to suggest that the change in attitude of noah's wife should also be included in this general picture. She may simply have thought that, with ham's wife gone, another should take her place, not in order to keep the widower company on his now solitary nights, but to recover the harmony enjoyed before among the younger females of the family and their guest cain, or, put more plainly, given that he had been used to having three women at his disposal, there was no reason why he should not continue to do so. Little did she know that the ideas going round and round in cain's head made this matter an entirely secondary one. Nevertheless, since one thing does not necessarily exclude the other, cain was

143

sympathetic to her advances, You may not believe it, she said, but despite my age, because I'm not exactly in the first flower of youth, and despite having borne three children, I still feel that I'm a desirable woman, what do you think, cain. It had stopped raining a long time ago, the great mass of water was now busily macerating the dead and pushing them gently, with its eternal rocking, into the mouths of the fish. Cain had gone to look out of the window to watch the sea shining in the moonlight, he had thought briefly about lilith and his son enoch, both of them now dead, but in a somewhat distracted manner, as if he didn't really care, and it was then that he heard that whispered voice beside him, You may not believe it. They went from there, he and she, into the cubicle where cain slept, they didn't even wait for noah, who was already lying in the arms of morpheus, to depart this world, and when they had finished, cain had to acknowledge that the woman had been right in her view of herself, she did still have plenty of go in her and, at certain moments, revealed an acrobatic quality that the other women did not, either through a lack of natural vocation, or because they were inhibited by their respective husbands' more traditional approach. And on the subject of husbands, we should mention that ham was the second person to disappear. He had gone up on deck to adjust some planks that were keeping him awake with their creaking, when someone came up to him, Can you give me a hand, ham asked, Yes, came the reply, and ham was hurled into the sea, a fall of some fifty feet, which, although it seemed interminable, was soon over. Noah blustered and raged, saying that after all that time on the boat, only an unforgivable lapse of attention could explain such an occurrence, Keep your eyes open, he said, watch where you're putting your feet, and he went on, We have lost one couple, which means we're going to have to copulate even more if we are to do god's will and become the fathers and mothers of the new human race. He broke off for a moment and, turning to his two remaining daughters-in-law, asked, Is either of you pregnant. One said yes, she was, the other that she wasn't yet sure, And who is the father, Well, I think it's cain, said japheth's wife, I do too, said shem's wife, Goodness me, said noah, if your husbands don't have the necessary generative power, then you had better just lie with cain, which is, in fact, what I foresaw would happen from the start. For reasons best known to themselves, the women, noah's wife included, smiled, while the men, who were most displeased by this public dressing-down, promised to try harder in future. It's odd how lightly people speak about the future, as if they held it in their hand, as if it was in their power to push it further off or bring it nearer in accordance with the needs and expediencies of the moment. Japheth, for example, sees the future as a succession of fruitful copulations, one child a year, a few twins now and then, with the lord gazing fondly down upon him, a lot of sheep, a lot of yokes of oxen, in short, happiness. The poor man does not know that his end is nigh, that he will be tripped up and thrown into the void with no life jacket on, gesticulating wildly and crying out in an agony of futile

145

despair as the ark proceeds majestically on to meet its destiny. The loss of yet another crew member caused noah indescribable distress, the realisation of the lord's plan was at grave risk, and, given the situation, they would have to double or even triple the time needed to achieve a reasonable repopulation of the earth. Cain's collaboration was becoming ever more important, which is why noah, since cain seemed unwilling to make the first move, decided to have a man-to-man talk with him, Enough of this beating about the bush, enough mincing of words, he said, from now on it's whenever and however, all these worries will be the death of me, and I can't be of much help for the moment, Whenever and however, repeated cain, what does that mean, Yes, and whoever too, answered noah, giving cain a knowing wink, Including your wife, asked cain, Yes, I insist on it, she's my wife and I can do with her as I wish, Especially since it's in a good cause, said cain, A sacred cause, the lord's cause, agreed noah in appropriately solemn tones, Well, in that case, let's start right away, said cain, send her to the cubicle where I sleep and tell the others not to disturb us, regardless of what happens or what noises you may hear, Certainly, and may the lord's will be done, Amen to that. Now some might think that mischievous cain was enjoying the situation, playing cat and mouse with his innocent companions, whom, as you will already have suspected, he has been eliminating one by one. They would be quite wrong. Cain is wrestling with his anger against the lord, as if he were caught in the tentacles of an octopus, and his latest victims are, as was abel in the past, merely further attempts on his part to kill god. His next victim will be noah's wife, who, quite undeservedly, will pay with her life for the hours of pleasure spent in the arms of her future assassin, and with the blessing and connivance of her own husband too, such was the dissolute nature of this race of humans whose final days we are witnessing. After repeated displays, with a few more or less subtle variations, of various wild, erotic deliriums, mainly on the part of the woman, and which found expression, as usual, in murmurs, moans and, finally, uncontrollable screams, cain led her by the hand to the window to enjoy the cool night air, and there he placed his hands between her still trembling thighs and heaved her into the sea. The only remaining members of noah's family of eight were the patriarch himself, his son shem and his wife and japheth's widow. Two women should still be enough, thought noah with his unfailing optimism and his unshakeable trust in the lord. However, he couldn't conceal his bewilderment at his wife's inexplicable disappearance and he said as much to cain, She was in your care, I just can't understand how such a misfortune could have happened, to which cain responded with a question, Was I your wife's keeper, did I have her tethered to me by the ankle with a rope, as if she were a sheep, No, no, I don't mean that, said noah, retreating slightly, but she was sleeping with you, and you might have noticed something, Yes, but I sleep very deeply. The conversation went no further, and it was true that cain could hardly be held responsible for the fact that noah's wife got up in the dark and went outside for a pee in the night breeze, and there perhaps, after suffering a dizzy spell, rolled to the side of the ship and vanished into the waters. Just one of those unfortunate things. The level of the vast sea covering the earth continued to subside, but no mountain peak had raised its head to say, Here I am, my name is ararat and I'm in turkey. Nevertheless, the great voyage was nearing its end, and it was time to prepare for the conclusion, the landfall or whatever it would be. Shem and his wife had both fallen into the sea in as yet unexplained circumstances, and the same had happened to japheth's widow, who had spent the previous night in cain's bed. Now noah was tearing his hair out in despair, all is lost, with no women to impregnate, there will be no life and no human race, it would have been far better to have made do with the familiar world they had, and he went on, distraught, How can I stand before the lord with nothing but this boatful of animals to show him, what shall I do, how will I live out the rest of my life, Throw yourself overboard, said cain, no angel will scoop you up in his arms. There was something in the way cain said this that awoke noah to reality, It was you, he said, Yes, it was me, answered cain, but I won't touch you, you will die by your own hand, And god, what will god say, asked noah, Don't worry, I'll take care of god. Noah took the six steps that separated him from the edge of the boat and, without another word, jumped.

The following day, the boat reached land. And the voice of god was heard, saying, Noah, noah, come forth from the ark with your wife and your sons and the wives of your sons, bring forth with you every living thing that is with you, both fowl and cattle and every creeping thing that creeps upon the earth, that they may breed abundantly on the earth and be fruitful and multiply. There was a silence, then the door of the ark slowly opened and the animals began to emerge. Out they came, an endless stream, some large, like the elephant and the hippopotamus, some small, like the lizard and the cricket, others medium-sized, like the goat and the sheep. When the tortoises, who were the last to emerge, were moving off, slowly and ponderously as is their way, god called, Noah, noah, why do you not come out. Emerging from the dark interior of the ark, cain appeared on the threshold of the great door, Where are noah and his family, asked the lord, They're all dead, answered cain, Dead, what do you mean, dead, how, Well, apart from noah, who drowned himself of his own free will, I killed them all, You murderer, how dare you ruin my plan, is this how you show your gratitude for my having spared your life when you killed abel, asked the lord, There had to come a day when someone would show you your true face, What about the new human race I had prom-ised, There was one, but there won't be another and no one will miss it, You are indeed cain, the vile, wicked killer of your own brother, Not as vile and wicked as you, remember the children in sodom. There was a great silence. Then cain said, Now you can kill me, No, I can't, the word of god cannot be taken back, you will die a natural death on the empty earth, and carrion birds will devour your flesh, Yes, once you have devoured my spirit. God's answer went unheard, and what cain said next was lost too, but it seems likely that they argued with each other on many other occasions, and one thing we know for certain is that they continued to argue and are arguing still. The story, though, is over, there will be nothing more to tell.

Translator's Acknowledgements

The translator would like to thank Tânia Ganho, Ben Sherriff and Euan Cameron for all their help and advice.